HOMECOMING TO MURDER

HOMECOMING TO MURDER
A Nathan Perry Mystery

CAROL PREFLATISH

Cover design: Stephen Zimmer

Cover art in this book copyright © 2020 Stephen Zimmer & Seventh Star Press, LLC.

Editor: Stephen Zimmer

Published by Seventh Star Press, LLC.

ISBN Number: 978-1-948042-96-3

Seventh Star Press

www.seventhstarpress.com

info@seventhstarpress.com

Publisher's Note:

Homecoming to Murder is a work of fiction. All names, characters, and places are the product of the author's imagination, used in fictitious manner. Any resemblances to actual persons, places, locales, events, etc. are purely coincidental.

Printed in the United States of America

First Edition

Acknowledgements

Special thanks to Seventh Star Press for believing in my journey to write mysteries.

Thanks also to my Q&Q and TOWG writing groups for all of their help.

Dedication

To my husband, who helped a lot with the police technicalities.

Chapter One

Tick-Tick-Tick. In the silence of the house, the sound from the large grandfather clock unnerved him. It showed eight P.M.

This is taking too long, he thought.

"Look at this." The younger of the two men held up a small gold-colored statue, showing it to the older man.

"Shut up and put it in the bag. Did you get the jewelry from upstairs?"

"Yeah."

"Let's get out of here then. We've been here too long already."

Frank looked around the room, jealous. People actually live with so many expensive items around their houses just collecting dust. He shook his head and picked up two bags, following the younger of the duo through the house to the rear door. In the kitchen, they froze in their steps when they heard the door to the garage being unlocked.

"What do we do?" Ricky, the younger of the two, asked.

There was no time for an answer. The door opened, and a man carrying a briefcase and computer bag walked in. He looked up and made eye contact with the one of the burglars. As he moved his eyes toward Ricky, the sound of the gunshot momentarily deafened them.

"What the hell!" his partner grabbed the gun. "What

were you thinking bringing a gun with you?"

"He saw your face and was about to see mine." The younger man puffed out his chest. "Motherfucker can't ID us now."

"You stupid bastard." He wanted to coldcock him with the butt of the gun, but stopped himself. "Come on. We got get out of here."

Picking up the computer bag, both men stepped over the body, doing their best to avoid the blood beginning to pool on the floor.

One month later

Memories started flooding back into Nathan Perry's mind as he drove into the city limits of his hometown of Mystic, Massachusetts. He'd been happy growing up here, a star football player with prospects of college scholarships and, inevitably, a pro career.

Things changed the summer after graduating high school, enough to make him leave town and never return, until now. Parking his truck at the Mystic Inn, he went inside to register. Tomorrow could either make or break the rest of his life.

The next morning, Nathan stared at himself in the mirror before departing for his appointment. It had been a long time since he wore a suit. After leaving Mystic, his life had been hard and adventurous, but he had kept himself in pretty good shape for a man of thirty years. The Army will do that to you. So far, no gray had found its way into his thick, dark brown hair.

Checking his watch, he had just enough time to stop for breakfast on the way to his interview. He straightened his tie, put on his coat, and left the room.

Outside, he shivered in the cold January air and buttoned his coat up to the neck in a feeble attempt to keep out the stinging breeze, which was standard for this ocean side town.

Even with the sun shining brightly, he felt the cold all the way to his bones. As he walked past the hardware store, he caught a glimpse of himself limping. It was better, but still there. Straightening up, he concentrated harder on hiding it.

With plenty of time before his appointment, he stopped by the café on the way to the police department. An early crowd had filled *The Witch's Brew* as he stood at the door looking for an empty table. Finally spotting one near the rear of the room, he started toward it.

"Nathan? Is that you?" a woman called from one of the booths.

He stopped where a well-dressed, shapely, brown-eyed brunette woman sat. Something about her seemed familiar, and then it came to him. "Dana Tyler?"

"Yes." With a big smile, she stood and they hugged. "I haven't seen you in years. What are you doing back in town?"

"I have a job interview," he said.

"Really? Why don't you sit down and tell me about it? We need to catch up."

Nathan slid into the opposite side of her booth. Dana had been his high school sweetheart, and his heart skipped a beat when he saw her. He glanced at her left hand and saw no wedding band. If he ended up moving back to Mystic, it might be nice knowing a single lady in town.

"So, job interview, eh? Does this mean you're moving back home?"

"If the job pans out, yes."

A waitress came up to the table. "I thought you said you were eating alone today, Dana. Who's your handsome friend?"

"I was, but an old high school friend showed up. This is Nathan Perry. Nathan, this is Ginger Raines. She owns this place."

"How do you do, Ms. Raines?"

"Oh honey, please don't call me that. I'm Ginger to everyone."

He wasn't sure how to take the flamboyant, slightly overweight woman with bright red spiked hair, but she seemed to accept him without reservation. "It's nice to meet you, Ginger. Please call me Nathan."

"What can I get you, Nathan?"

He picked up the laminated, single sheet menu perched behind the napkin holder and gave it a quick look. "I'll have the breakfast sandwich and cup of coffee."

"I'll be right back." Ginger turned and headed to the kitchen.

"Tell me about this interview," Dana asked.

"It's for the detective job with the Mystic Police Department."

"Really? I knew they were hiring, but I had no idea they were looking outside the department to fill it."

"I wouldn't know about that, but the Chief of Police called me last week to schedule an interview."

"So, you're a police officer?"

"Not right now. I was Military Police in the Army, but left the service some time ago. What are you doing now?"

"I'm the lead reporter for *The Mystic Messenger*. I've actually been covering the story about the hiring of the new detective. I should have known they were looking outside of Mystic." She took out a notebook.

He watched her scribble something. "You're not going to write about me in the newspaper, are you?"

She looked up from her notes. "Well, if you're hired, it's news."

"Dana, I haven't even had my interview yet and for them to think I'm talking to the press beforehand could ax my whole chance."

"Here you go, breakfast sandwich and coffee," Ginger said, interrupting the conversation. "Can I get either of you anything else?"

"No, thanks," Nathan said. Dana shook her head.

Ginger cleared away Dana's dishes and left Nathan's

check on the table before walking away.

Nathan took a bite of his sandwich.

"I wouldn't write anything that would jeopardize your chances. It would be great to have you back in town."

She smiled and he wasn't sure, but she may have blushed a little. He swallowed. "I think I'd like living back here again."

"Where have you been living? When I came home from college for Christmas, you were nowhere to be found."

"After my parents were killed in October in that auto accident, I needed to get away, so I joined the Army. I got out a couple years ago and have been living in Washington, D.C. since." He wasn't sure how much more he wanted to tell her, not because she was a reporter, but because he didn't want to share too much about his life just yet.

"What were you doing in Washington? You know, for a living."

There it was, the question he had hoped to avoid. "Nothing. I had saved up enough money that I didn't need to work." Nathan took another bite and wiped his mouth with the napkin. He looked at his watch and swallowed. "I really need to go." He took a drink of his coffee and picked up the check.

"You've barely touched your food."

"I don't want to be late for my interview." He reached for his wallet.

"Let me get that for you, for old times sake." Dana took the check out of his hand.

"I can't let you do that."

"I insist. You can get dinner next time," she said with a wink.

"Okay, thanks. I'll do that." He put some dollar bills down on the table for the tip.

"Here's my card. Call me." She placed her card into his hand.

"If I end up moving back here, you'll be my first call. It was nice seeing you again, Dana."

"It was great seeing you, too. Good luck with your interview," she said.

He turned and left the café.

Outside, he continued his walk to the Mystic Police Department. The two-story brick building was only four-blocks away. Standing in front of the building, his thoughts went back to his teenage years, when he used to drive by wondering what it looked like inside. Luckily, he had never gotten into enough trouble back then that it warranted him seeing the inside.

Walking up the steps, he took a deep breath and opened the glass door, stepping inside. In front of him stood a counter with several officers working behind it. On the wall behind them hung a large wooden town seal with a silhouette of a witch riding a broom on it. Two benches on each side of the door had people sitting and waiting, possibly for the same interview that he was there for.

"Can I help you?" a female officer from behind the counter asked.

He stepped up. "I'm Nathan Perry. I have an appointment with Chief Cabot."

The officer typed something on the computer and then looked back at Nathan. "If you'll have a seat, I'll tell him you're here."

"Thank you."

Instead of sitting, he felt like pacing. He needed this job. It had been a long twenty-four months and he was finally ready to get back to work. It was only by chance that he found out about the detective position after doing an Internet search of his hometown.

Moving back could be just the medicine he needed. Walking from his hotel to the police department this morning, he saw how so much had changed since his high school days, and he welcomed the chance to learn the town all over again.

"Mr. Perry."

"Yes." He walked over to the older man wearing a police

uniform.

"I'm Paul Cabot, Chief of Police." The two men shook hands.

"It's nice to meet you, Chief Cabot. I've been looking forward to this interview."

"If you'll follow me to my office, we'll get started."

As he and the chief walked down the hallway, they passed several of the department's officers. Nathan thought he might have recognized a few from his youth, but it had been so long ago, he wasn't sure.

They stepped onto the elevator and the chief pushed the button for the second floor. When the doors opened, he followed the chief around the corner to his office.

"Right in here, Mr. Perry. Please sit down," Chief Cabot said, closing the door and then sitting behind his desk. "Would you like some coffee?"

"No, thank you."

"I suppose I should fill you in on the job. The Mystic PD has never had a detective or an investigative unit, but with the increase of tourists spilling over from Salem, crime is on the increase. The mayor decided that we needed at least one detective to work on certain crimes, with the possibility of hiring more later."

"Tourist season around here used to be a summer only event. What about the rest of the time, would I still be a detective or transferred to patrol?" Nathan asked.

"The detective position would be a year-round position." The chief took a drink from his coffee cup. "I was very impressed with your law enforcement experience in the Army. Can you elaborate a little more than what was on your resume?"

"I was an MP in the Army for five of my eight years. The last three years, I was a Special Agent with the Criminal Investigative Command. Two and half years was in Afghanistan."

"You've been out of the Army for a couple years. What

have you been doing for that time?"

He couldn't avoid it any longer. Lying at a job interview would be the kiss of death and he wanted this job. "While in Afghanistan, I was injured and have been recuperating for the last two years."

"Injured? What type of injury? I would need to make sure it's not something that would hamper your ability on the job." Chief Cabot sat back in his chair awaiting the answer.

"I had been sent to a nearby town to investigate some thefts from the camp. The vehicle I traveled in hit an IED. I suffered a ruptured ear membrane and a fractured leg."

"You're a lucky man."

"Yes, sir. I think about that every day. I eventually ended up at Walter Reed to recover from the fracture and my hearing loss. It took two surgeries and a lot of therapy, but my hearing finally returned to normal and my fractured leg has mended, although I do limp on occasion. I brought a medical statement for you from the hospital." Nathan took a folded sheet of paper from the breast pocket of his jacket and handed it to the chief.

The chief took the paper and looked it over. "Everything seems in order. However, I would like for you to have a physical with our department physician just to make sure you meet all of our requirements."

"That's no problem. Thank you."

"Why have you decided to come back to Mystic? I'm sure you could work at any top-notch security agency around."

"I've been living in Washington for the last two years. I always liked the slower pace of a small town, even though as a teenager living here, I never realized that. It was time to leave the city and come back. I saw this job listed on the internet. I thought it was a good fit."

Chief Cabot nodded and took a few minutes to again look over Nathan's resume. "I think you would be an asset for this department, Mr. Perry. You're a hometown boy and you've got the training and experience we need. I'd like to offer you the job on a trial basis."

"Trial basis?" Nathan questioned. "How long of a trial basis?"

"It would be sort of a probation period and the length depends on how well you do. We've had a series of unsolved burglaries on Mano Island recently. The last one resulted in a murder. I need for you to solve these cases. If you can do that, then you'll be hired permanently."

"You're serious. Solve the murder, I'm hired. Don't solve it and I'm fired."

"I'm afraid that's the offer. If you accept the position, I'd like for you to start on Monday."

Nathan thought over the offer. What choice did he have? He really wanted to move back to his hometown, and good paying jobs were as scarce here as anywhere. "I'll take it. Oh, and one thing."

"What's that?"

"I'd like to keep my injuries private. They don't hamper me in any way, but others might think otherwise."

"You have nothing to worry about. That will be a personnel matter and only I'll know."

"Thank you, sir. I appreciate that."

"Be back here by eight o'clock Monday morning."

"I'm looking forward to it."

Nathan walked out of the police department and let out a sign of relief. *One task down, one to go*, he thought.

He needed to get his parents' old home opened back up so he could move in. Before going back to his hotel room, he stopped by the electric and water companies to make sure those utilities were on and transferred from his sister's name into his.

The next morning, Nathan checked out of the hotel, but before going to his parents' home, he stopped by the hardware store to purchase a few tools and some supplies.

Placing his items on the counter to pay, he suddenly heard a woman's booming voice. "Nathaniel? Nathaniel

Perry?" He recognizing the voice immediately and reluctantly turned. "It that you, Nathaniel. What on earth are you doing back in Mystic? I thought I'd be dead and buried before you ever came back here."

The woman rushed over and, with her bright red painted lips, planted a big kiss right on his cheek. He rubbed his face, knowing there had to be a lipstick stain there. Aunt Agnes was his father's sister who never married and was always forthcoming with kisses. She was a bold woman, and he had vivid childhood memories of he and his sister at family dinners with Aunt Agnes trying to play games with them and their cousins.

"Hello, Aunt Agnes. I thought you lived in Florida?"

"I do, but I had to come back here to take care of some business. You're lucky you caught me. I'll be going back to Tampa in a few days. You didn't answer my question. What are you doing in Mystic? Aren't you still in the Navy?"

"It was the Army and I got out a while ago. I'm moving back to Mystic."

"Oh, I wish we could get together for dinner with your sister, but my days are just jammed full of things to do before I leave."

"Maybe the next time you come back," he suggested.

"I'll definitely look you up. Are you going to live at your folks' place on the coast?"

"Yes, ma'am."

"Good. I hated seeing that place sit empty for so long." She looked at her watch. "I must be going. You tell your sister hello for me." She planted another red kiss on his other cheek and started toward the door."

"I will, Aunt Agnes." Nathan wiped his face again. He was sure he looked like a clown now. As he looked at the hardware clerk, he saw she was doing her best to keep from laughing.

Nathan spent the whole weekend getting the house cleaned up and minor repairs made. It had been eight years since anyone lived at the ocean side home. While a caretaker cut the grass in the summer, not much else had been done to the property, which also included an old lighthouse. The repairs that needed to be made would take a lot longer than the weekend, but at least he could get enough done to move in.

By noon on Saturday, Nathan had replaced the locks on all of the doors and windows and fixed a leak in the bathroom. He was just about to crawl under the kitchen sink when he heard a knock at the door. Curious as to who would be visiting, he walked to the front of the house.

Through the door's window, he immediately recognized the woman. "Dana, what are you doing here?"

"I heard you got the job. When you weren't at your hotel, I took a chance you'd be out here." She held up a sack. "I brought sandwiches from town, if you need a lunch break?"

"I sure do. Come in." He opened the door wider so she could enter. "How did you know which hotel I was staying at?"

"Reporter, remember?" She followed him into the kitchen. "It's been a long time since I was in this house."

"If my memory is right, it was my high school graduation party," he said.

"You remember?"

"I do. I'm sorry I don't have much furniture yet. It won't be delivered until next week. I'm afraid all I have is this folding table and these two chairs."

"That's fine." She took the sandwiches out of the bag as Nathan cleared the table of tools and papers.

"Can I get you a bottle of water?"

"Yes, please." She walked over to the sliding doors that looked out onto the ocean. "I forgot how nice the view is here. I remember how we used to sit for hours on those big rocks next to the lighthouse."

That reminded Nathan of high school and their time spent together. Both were so young and thought they were in love. She had turned into a beautiful woman, one that he might enjoy getting to know all over again.

"Hey, how about that water?" she said, bringing him back to reality.

"Right. Here you go." He opened the lid to the cooler sitting on the counter and handed her a cold, dripping bottle, which she dried with a napkin. He got one for himself and sat down at the table with her. "I don't have a refrigerator yet."

"Are you going to stay out here until your furniture arrives?" she asked.

"Yes." He unwrapped one of the sandwiches and took a drink.

"Where are you going to sleep?"

Nathan laughed. I bought a cot at the hardware store." He motioned toward the living room and she got up to take a look.

"It looks terribly uncomfortable for an all night sleep."

"I've slept on worse," he said, remembering some of his nights in Afghanistan.

She returned to the kitchen table and opened her sandwich.

"I forgot to congratulate you on getting the job at the police department. I'm glad you got it."

"Thanks. I'm glad to be back in Mystic."

"When do you start?" She took a sip of water.

"Monday morning."

"I'd love to do an interview with you for the newspaper. I'm sure the readers would like to know what you've been up to since you left town."

"No."

"What do you mean, no?"

"I don't want my life spread across the front page," he said.

Dana laughed. "Well, aren't you full of yourself. Believe me, even in Mystic, you wouldn't be front page material."

Nathan couldn't help but laugh, too. "I still don't want to be in the paper, not yet."

"But Nathan, this is news."

"No." He got up and walked to the sliding door. "I appreciate the food, but I really need to get back to work. I only have today and tomorrow to get the house fixed up as much as I can before my furniture gets here later this week."

"Of course, I understand." She got up, put her coat on, and rewrapped her sandwich to take with her.

"Thanks again for bringing lunch," he said.

"You're welcome." She started toward the front door.

She sounded mad and he knew he needed to make amends before she left. "Would you like to have dinner later this week?"

She stopped and turned toward him. "Really?" She seemed hesitant.

"Yes. I owe you a dinner, remember?"

"That would be nice."

"I'm not sure what my schedule will be yet, but as soon as I know something, I'll give you a call. I still have your card."

She smiled. "I'll look forward to it."

He opened the door for her, and she walked out, not looking back as she called, "Bye."

Chapter Two

Early Monday morning, Nathan walked into the police department, finding the front lobby fairly empty except for the officers working at the counter. But it was early. The same female officer with auburn hair greeted him as she had done on Friday.

"Good morning. Can I help you?" she asked.

"I'm Nathan Perry. I'm the new detective starting today."

The sounds of shuffling papers, conversations, and typing on keyboards stopped, and Nathan became painfully aware of the virtual spotlight now on him.

"Oh, of course. The chief said you'd be starting today. If you'll come with me, I'll show you to your office, Detective," she said, standing.

He followed her down the hallway. "Please, call me Nathan. I don't really like titles that well."

"Okay, Nathan. I'm Gloria Wheeler, patrol officer, but I mostly manage the front desk."

Nathan had already noticed that she wore a sidearm accompanied by an expert marksman pin above her pocket.

"Here we are. This is your office. It's pretty bare right now, but I suspect you'll fill it up quick enough."

"Thank you, " he replied.

"The breakroom is down that hallway on the left." She pointed to the hall across from Nathan's office. "The employee restrooms can be found there also. Down the hall and past the breakroom are two interrogation rooms and the briefing room is across from the breakroom. In the back of the building is booking and on the second floor, you'll find the administrative offices and of course the chief's office. There's more to the building, but you can take a tour yourself. I'll let the chief know you're here. Oh, and the morning briefing is in about twenty minutes. You might want to grab some coffee before going in. You do drink coffee, right?"

"Couldn't function without it. I'll be there. Thanks, Gloria."

She left. Nathan took off his coat and sat at his desk, studying the office. Besides his desk and chair, the small square-shaped room held two file cabinets, a bookcase, and two old wooden, straight-backed chairs facing his desk.

Gloria hit the nail on the head when she said bare. Freshly painted white walls surrounded him, except for a set of three windows that circled behind his desk and overlooked the department's rear parking area. A small clock hung on the wall across from this desk.

When his stuff from D.C. arrived, he would bring in his certificates, photos, and desk set for the office. He made a mental note to call his former girlfriend, Katherine, and make sure his photos, certificates, and books were packed with his furniture for shipping.

"Perry, glad to see you're here," Chief Cabot said from the doorway.

"Yes, sir." Nathan quickly stood. "I'm anxious to get started."

"Good, happy to hear it. Please sit down."

Nathan sat and the chief came in, handing him a case file before sitting down. "This is your first case."

Nathan opened the file and started looking through it.

The chief continued, "That's the file for the burglaries and murder."

"There were some pretty expensive items stolen."

"Yes, mostly jewelry and electronics. The last theft was five days ago," the chief said. "That's when the murder occurred. We believe the homeowner walked in on the burglary and was killed."

That disturbed Nathan. "I don't see any leads or suspects listed in the file."

That's because we don't have any and why I hired you. I need you to solve this case."

That sounded simple enough, but with no leads in three months, Nathan feared this case might make for a short career. A knock at the door broke his thoughts. He looked up and saw Gloria.

"Gentlemen, the morning briefing is about to begin," she said.

"We'll be right there, Gloria," the chief said and then looked at Nathan. "One more thing before we go to the briefing." The chief stood. From of his pocket, he pulled a shiny gold detective badge and holder, placing it on the desk.

Nathan picked it up. "Thank you, sir."

"It's brand new. Don't disappoint me. Before you leave today, you need to get your department I.D. made. They can do that in the booking room."

"Yes, sir." Nathan stood and attached the badge to his belt, then followed Chief Cabot to the briefing room. Once inside with the other officers, the chief stopped to say something to the shift sergeant, and then he stood next to Nathan at the rear of the room.

With the room holding about twelve officers, the sergeant moved to the front of the room and began the morning briefing by going over the log sheets from the previous night shift. He mentioned a couple of street closures, the day's weather report, and then he turned the meeting over to the chief who stepped to the front of the room. All of the officers stood as he walked to the podium.

"Good morning. Please be seated. I suppose you all know that I'm here to talk to you again about the Mano Island burglaries. The insurance companies aren't too happy about paying so many claims and with tourist season not that far away, the mayor is on my back about making an arrest for the murder. That brings me to my announcement."

He motioned for Nathan to join him. "This is Nathan Perry, our new detective, and his first case will be to find who is committing these crimes." Nathan walked to the front of the room. There were a few mumbles of welcome and a couple weak handclaps. The chief stepped back and waved his arm toward the podium. Nathan stepped forward.

"Thank you, Chief Cabot." He looked at the group of officers and wondered what they really thought of him. Had he taken the detective job right out from under one or more of them? Would he get any cooperation from the officers, or even be accepted by them? "Mystic is my hometown. I grew up here, went to high school here, and then left for the Army. I came back because I love this town and want a new start. The chief just gave me the case file a few minutes before we stepped in here, so I've only taken a quick glance at it. I'm not a superhero that's going to be able to swoop in and solve it in a matter of minutes. It's going to take teamwork, so I hope I can count on the whole department to help. Thank you."

With the room still silent, the chief stepped back up to the podium. "I would like to assign at least one officer to assist Detective Perry in his investigation. Would any of you like to volunteer?"

"I'd be happy to help, Chief," Gloria said.

"Thank you, Gloria. I was already counting on your help with the paperwork, but I'd like to have a patrol officer," the chief said.

A few chuckles could be heard in the room. Whether the chief had meant to do so or not, he had insulted her status as an officer in front of her peers. Nathan had a feeling it was the chief's intention, and he couldn't help but notice how mad Gloria looked.

"I'll help," a male voice from the rear of the room said,

and an officer stood up.

He looked familiar, but Nathan couldn't place who he was.

"Thank you, Officer McCoy," Chief Cabot said. "I appreciate your offer. Please check with Detective Perry after the briefing. Oh, and you will still be expected to complete your regular patrols even with the additional assignment."

"Yes, sir."

Nathan began to realize that Chief Cabot might not be as pleasant and nice as he came across in the interview.

The sergeant stepped back to the podium. That's it for the morning briefing. Everybody hit the streets."

The officers stood and quickly left the room. Officer McCoy stayed behind and approached Nathan. "Hank McCoy," he said, extending his hand.

Nathan shook hands, trying to recall him from his past. "It seems like I should know you."

"We went to high school and played football together."

He thought for a moment and then smiled. "You played second string running back, right?"

"And, you played first string wide receiver, best player we ever had. You still hold the record for most yardage and passes received," McCoy said.

"Records aren't important. I remember you now. You were a couple years behind me in school. How the hell are you doing?" Nathan slapped him on the back, glad to find a connection to the past.

"I'm doing great. I've been with the department for six years now," Hank said.

The chief stood at the door and cleared his throat. "I hate to break this reunion up, but don't you two think you need to start working on the case?"

"Yes, sir. Just as soon as I find a cup of coffee, I plan on doing just that," Nathan said.

"Come on, the coffee's across the hall," Hank said, guiding him out of the room.

The chief remained silent and followed them out, but turned toward the elevator in the hallway.

Hank and Nathan walked into the break room and found Gloria standing by the coffee pot waiting for it to fill up. She looked up at them. "If either of you reach for that pot before me, you'll be pulling back a bloody stump."

"She means it, too," Hank said.

"I believe it. What's with the chief?"

Hank snickered. "You learn fast. He's taken a lot of heat over these burglaries and especially the murder."

"From who?"

"Mainly from the mayor," Gloria said. "But, the Homeowners Association on Mano Island is giving him a pretty hard time about it too. Not to mention, he doesn't think I can do anything but answer phones and do paperwork."

"Yeah, what about his comment to you?" Nathan asked.

With the pot of coffee filled, Gloria poured some into her cup. "He doesn't think women should be on patrolling. We're only good for paperwork, answering phones, and bringing him coffee and I'll be damned if I'm going to bring him any more coffee."

"Gloria, you know no one else in the department thinks that way," Hank said. He looked at Nathan. "You won't find a better or more knowledgeable officer than Gloria. She'd take a bullet for you."

She laughed. "Just don't put me between a bullet and the chief," she whispered.

Nathan didn't really think she meant it, at least he hoped not. With their cups filled with coffee, the three of them walked back to Nathan's office.

Gloria stopped at his door. "If you need me for anything, I'm at extension 110. Just give me a call."

"Thanks. I will," Nathan said.

"As long as it's not for coffee," she called as she walked down the hall.

The two men stepped into Nathan's office and sat down.

"She's a real spitfire," Nathan said.

"But, a damn smart officer. It's too bad the chief won't recognize it."

"She married?"

"Yes, her husband is the high school technology teacher and football coach," Hank said.

"No kidding. I'll have to make sure I get to some games next season."

"So, where do we start?" Hank asked.

"Tell me what you know about the burglaries," Nathan said.

"Well, you probably remember that Mano Island is where the more affluent from Mystic live. It appears whoever is doing this knows what houses have security systems and which ones don't. The homeowners are never home when break-ins occur and we can't figure out how they're getting in and out without being seen," Hank said. "We don't know for sure what happened with Mr. Miller, but we think he got home early and surprised the burglar. He was shot just inside the kitchen door."

Nathan studied the file. "Did he have a security system?"

"He didn't."

"Gloria mentioned something about a Homeowners Association. What can you tell me about them?"

"The president of the group is Quentin Mahoney. He's been the most vocal about it all. He works in Boston as a banker or something like that."

"Do you know when the group meets again?"

"No, but we can find out." Hank pushed the speaker button on Nathan's phone and dialed Gloria's extension.

"I knew you'd be calling," she said.

"It's Hank, Gloria."

"Oh."

"Can you see if you can find out when the next Homeowners Association's meeting is being held out on Mano Island?"

"Certainly. I'm the queen of the telephone, remember?"

"Right," he laughed. "Let us know when you find out."

Nathan looked though the case file. "There's been six burglaries and the murder so far, but they're all under one case number? That's really confusing and I bet the insurance companies didn't like getting reports that were mixed together."

"They've not been happy about anything with these cases," Hank said. "Without having a detective to run the investigation, whoever got the call wrote the report and stuck it in the same file. I don't think they've even been entered on the computer system yet."

"That is going to have to change."

Gloria appeared at the door holding her coffee cup. "The Association has a meeting tomorrow night."

"Thanks," Nathan said.

"Don't hesitate to call, if you need anything else," she said, heading to the break room.

"It's been a long time since I've been out to Mano Island. I'd like to go out and look around."

"My patrol car's out back. I'd be glad to drive," Hank said. "Besides, I can count that as some of my patrol time."

"Good, but first I need to ask Gloria to do something for me." Nathan picked up the case file. He then started looking through the drawers of his desk. "There's nothing in here, no pens, no paper, nothing."

"This actually used to be a storage room. The chief had it cleaned out and the desk, chairs, and file cabinets moved in for you. You're lucky to have a phone and computer in here," Hank said.

"Lucky? I don't know how to use the phone system yet and I haven't been given a login ID or password for the computer."

"I'll take you to the IT tech when we get back," Hank said.

Nathan grabbed his jacket and headed out the door and up the hallway toward the lobby with Hank following. They found Gloria back at the front counter.

"Hank and I are going to patrol Mano Island. Could I ask you to do two things for me?"

"That depends on what you need," she said.

"It's not coffee," Nathan joked back. "Could you go through this case file and make a separate file for each burglary with its own case number? There needs to be six individual cases instead of one."

"Sure, I can do that," she said. "But, why individual cases?"

"When we catch who's doing this, if we have separate cases, the District Attorney will be able to file separate charges for each burglary and the murder and it's a good way to compare each case for similarities too."

"That makes sense. I never thought about that," Hank said.

"You said two things. What's the other?" she asked.

"I don't have any office supplies. I need a small notebook and pen to take with me."

She opened her drawer and handed Nathan just what he needed. "I'll see that you get some other supplies by the time you get back."

"Thanks. You're going to be a big help with this investigation."

As they left, Nathan heard Gloria say, "Finally, some real police work for me." He smiled as he and Hank headed back down the hall toward the rear of the building.

"My patrol car is over here," Hank said, once outside. The two men got in and Hank drove out into traffic. "Where are you living?"

"I moved into my folks' old place out at the lighthouse, but my furniture and stuff haven't been delivered from D.C. yet. I'm hoping the movers will have everything here soon. It's a real pain in the ass to be out there without furniture."

"I bet it is. That house has sat empty for a long time."

"Yeah, and you can tell it, too. I've still got some things to fix out there."

"If you need any help or want to borrow some tools, let me know. I'd be glad to give you a hand."

"Thanks. I appreciate the offer and may take you up on that."

They drove out of downtown Mystic and along the highway. Nathan had always enjoyed the drive to Mano Island and it was still just as beautiful today. With the ocean running along one side of the road, it made for a great view. Although, with it being the middle of winter, the coastline was pretty bare.

Once they crossed the bridge to the island, they passed many luxury homes and he thought about how those homes were way past what his pay grade would ever be. All the homes had pools, tennis courts, and a few along the ocean even had their own private boat docks.

Nathan wondered how the officers that patrolled this area felt about watching over the people that had it all. Until the burglaries started, the worst crime on the island was probably a fender bender between two Bentleys.

"Which homes were burglarized?" Nathan asked.

Hank drove by each one, pointing them out to Nathan. "This last one right here is where Mr. Miller was murdered."

"Is it still considered a crime scene?"

"No, all of the evidence has been collected and a company came in a couple days ago to get it all cleaned up. Mrs. Miller is out of town with family right now, but should be home soon."

As they passed each one, Nathan looked at the homes that Hank continued to point out. "Three of the homes have their own boat docks and two of them are directly across the road from homes with boat docks." He wrote something on his notepad.

"Do you think that's how they're getting on and off the island without being seen?"

"Could be, but this time of year would sure be a cold ride in a boat."

"With the loot they're taking, they probably figure it's

worth it."

Having completed their patrol of the island, they headed back toward the bridge to Mystic. "Things haven't changed much on the island since I've been gone."

"It's changed more than you think. Many of the people that live out there aren't even originally from here. They've moved here from Boston," Hank said.

"Did they build new houses or buy existing ones?"

A little of both, but mostly bought the houses that were for sale and then remodeled."

"What happened to the people that were selling them?"

"A lot of them were older, retired, and moved to Florida for the warmer weather."

"Good retirement plan, I'll have to remember that," Nathan chuckled. "Is there a block watch or anything like that out here?"

"Only the Homeowners Association, as far as I know. Ryan Avery is the officer that patrols the island. He could tell you more about that." They crossed the bridge leaving the island. "Where to now?" Hank asked.

"Back to the department. I need to get my office set up."

After returning to the station, Nathan walked into his office alone, as Hank had to continue with his patrol shift. He tossed his pocket-sized notebook onto the desk and sat down. The day only half over, it seemed as if he'd already put in a whole day.

He hadn't had lunch yet and could use something to drink. Getting up, he went to the break room to get a soda. Just as he started to step back into his office, he saw Gloria walking toward him.

"Nathan, I didn't know you were back."

They both entered his office. "I've been back for about ten minutes. I guess I should let you know when I'm in, right?"

"It does help if the front counter people know when you're in or out. Here are the separated case files, labeled, and indexed with individual case numbers. Just like you asked."

He took the files from her and sat down. "You work fast. Thank you." He looked through the files.

"I love doing things like this. All I ever do is answer the phone and take care of complaints at the front. Do you know I have the same training as the patrol officers, but the chief won't let me or any of the other female officers do anything other than desk jobs?"

"Desk jobs are important too and from the looks of these files, you do a very good job. These files are perfect." Looking up and seeing the expression on her face, he quickly added, "but it's not right to treat the female officers differently."

"Thank you. I'm glad you agree." She sat down. "Since the chief said I could help you, I was hoping that you might have something I could do out in the field for the investigation."

Nathan realized that he might have put his foot in his mouth. "I'm sure there will be something you can do, but right now I need to read the individual files before I decide how to proceed."

"Okay, just remember, I really want to help with these cases. Oh, I have a box of office supplies for you. I'll be right back." She rushed out of the office.

Nathan put his soda on the desk, sat back in his chair, and swiveled around to look out of the window. He had forgotten how gray and dreary winters could be in Mystic. The overcast day made it look even colder outside.

He heard a knock at the door.

"Thanks, Gloria. Just set the supplies on my desk."

"Ah, it's not Gloria," a baritone voice replied.

Nathan turned to find an officer standing at the door and noticed the lieutenant bars on his collar. "I'm sorry. I was expecting Gloria with my office supplies."

"I'm Lieutenant Mark Matthews."

Nathan stood and the two men shook hands. "Nathan Perry. What can I do for you, Lieutenant?"

"The chief said one case wasn't enough for you." The lieutenant dropped a pile of folders on Nathan's desk. "I hand-picked these myself."

"Thanks." He noticed that the lieutenant was looking up and down at him.

"You're not wearing a sidearm."

"No, sir. I haven't had one issued to me yet."

"I'll inform Sgt. Richards. He's in charge of the armory. He'll be in touch before the end of the day."

"Thank you."

Gloria now stood at the door holding a box. Lieutenant. Matthews left, walking past her and not saying anything. Stepping into the office, she put the box on the desk next to the files.

"You know what he's doing, don't you?" she asked.

"Apparently not."

"Those files will be the most ridiculous cases we've had. The lieutenant and the other guys are going to send you on some wild goose chases. Go on, look through them." She said, sitting down.

Nathan picked up the first file, skimmed through it, and then laughed.

"I told you," she said. "How bad is it?"

"UFO," he said. "Someone spotted a UFO over the harbor north of town on three consecutive nights. On those same nights, several dogs disappeared."

"They'll all be complaints like that. Don't waste your time on them."

Nathan still had a smile on his face. "This is great."

"Great? You think it's great you got the crazy cases?"

"I was afraid I wouldn't be accepted by the other officers, but pulling something like this proves me wrong. They are willing to give me a chance."

"You're a remarkable man," Gloria said, shaking her head.

"I am?"

"Most men would have gotten mad and marched into the LT's office throwing those cases in his face, but instead you saw it for the joke it was."

"Thank you, Gloria."

She blushed and stood. "Oh, I almost forgot. I put instructions in the box on how to use the phone system and Mallory, our IT tech, brought your login ID and password for the computer while you were gone. It's in there, too."

"Thanks. Hank was going to help me get those, but he had to get back on patrol," he said, as she left the room.

A clerk came by with payroll and benefit forms to fill out, and he spent the next several hours at his desk doing paperwork. After that, he read through the rest of the cases from the lieutenant. Nathan was happy to discover that at least some of them involved actual crimes.

Sitting back in his chair, he rubbed his eyes. Reading case files all afternoon had really put a strain on them. He needed a break and figured this would be a good time to tour the building, second floor first.

Stepping off of the elevator onto the second floor, he walked down the hallway. Offices lined along both walls. He passed the chief's open office door and saw him and another man sitting inside.

"Perry!"

Nathan stopped and went back.

"Detective, come in. There's someone here I want you to meet. This is Mayor Robert Newcomb. Bob, this is our new detective, Nathan Perry."

Newcomb stood and, like any politician, extended his hand. Nathan first noticed how young he seemed to be for a mayor and wondered what kind of connections he had to gain that powerful position.

Nathan shook his hand. "How do you do, sir?"

Newcomb stood a little over six foot with brown hair and brown eyes. Nathan noticed he was a sharp dresser and was sure he was wearing a designer suit, nothing like the one he bought at J.C. Penney.

"Wonderful to meet you, detective. I understand you're working on the Mano Island murder," Newcomb said.

"Yes, sir, and the burglaries as well."

"Of course. How is it going?"

"Well, this is just my first day, so I'm mainly familiarizing myself with the cases I've been assigned. I'm sure I'll have something on the Mano Island case soon," Nathan said, giving him the standard answer when nothing has been moving forward on a case.

"I'll be expecting an update soon. The Mystic Police Department can't let a murderer run loose on our streets. It's too dangerous and bad for the tourist business."

And, I'm sure it's an election year and you don't want to lose votes, Nathan thought. "Everyone's doing their best, sir. Now, if you will excuse me, I have a few things I need to finish up before the end of the day."

He left the office and looked around the rest of the floor before taking the stairs back down, deciding to see what was in the basement. On the walk down, he thought about Newcomb. It seemed that all he cared about were the tourists. Keep the tourists coming made business owners happy, resulting in votes on Election Day. Nathan hated politics, but with this job, he'd have to play along for a little while.

At the bottom of the stairs, he opened the door and found himself next to the armory. Now being as good of a time as any, he stepped up to the window. "Excuse me, I'm Nathan Perry and I'm looking for Sgt. Richards."

"I'm Richards," one of the officers behind the window said.

"I just started today as the new detective and need to get a sidearm issued to me."

"Oh yes, Detective Perry. Lieutenant Matthews told me about you. What's your preference?"

"I used a Smith and Wesson 9mm in the Army with a belt holster," he answered.

"I think we can fix you up. Be right back," the sergeant said.

Nathan took note of the armory. Behind the glass window

looked like Richards' office. One other officer sat to the left, working on a gun at the bench where the tools were hanging on a pegboard. He was sure the room the officer went into held a vault with all the weapons in it.

A few minutes later, the officer returned carrying a box. He slid open the window and handed Nathan the pistol, grip first. Taking the gun, he first made sure it wasn't loaded. Extending his arm at eye level, he checked the sight and then dry-fired it once to check the trigger function. "I think this will work just fine." He handed the gun back to the sergeant.

"Let me get the numbers off of the gun and I'll have you sign it out," the sergeant said. He started filling out the form. "How much ammo do you want?"

"I'll take a box of cartridges to start. Does the department have a firing range?"

"We do. It's on the west side of town. When you want to go, let me know and you can sign out a key."

Nathan read over the form that Sgt. Richards handed him and signed it.

"Thank you, detective. Here's your weapon, holster, and ammo. Welcome to the department."

"Thanks, sergeant. I'm glad to be here."

Nathan took his new equipment and went back to his office where he loaded the gun. He checked his watch and saw that it was four o'clock. "Time to go home."

Before leaving, Nathan noticed a light on his phone flashing. Sitting down at this desk, he got out the instructions that Gloria had given him on how to check his voicemail. The only message was from Dana Tyler. "Nathan, it's Dana. I was wondering if you have a statement for the paper about the break-ins and murder on Mano Island? Call me."

He would call her back, but it could wait until tomorrow. Nathan was tired and hungry. Still, he didn't feel like cooking tonight, not to mention he didn't have anything much to cook with, so he thought he'd stop by Capt's Waterfront Grill for a sandwich and drink.

The restaurant was on his way home and it didn't take long for Nathan to drive there. He walked in and immediately saw Dana sitting alone at the bar.

He slid onto the bar stool next to her. "Want some company?" he asked.

"Always, when it's you. Long first day?"

"It was."

The bartender walked over and Dana introduced Nathan. "Scott, this is Nathan Perry, the new police detective in town. Nathan, this is Scott Reid. He runs this place."

"Glad to meet you," Nathan said.

"You, too. What can I get you?"

"Beer on tap, please, and a menu." He turned to Dana, noticing she nursed a single drink. "You meeting someone tonight?"

"No, just stopped for a drink on the way home."

"Yeah, me too."

Scott sat a tall frosty glass of beer in front of Nathan and handed him a menu. "Can I get you another glass of Chablis, Miss Tyler?"

Nathan spoke up before she could. "Bring her another glass and we'll take it at a table." He stood and Dana followed his lead, and they walked to a table across the room next to the window overlooking the harbor.

"So, anything yet the Mano Island crimes?" she asked.

Nathan had to be careful when he talked with Dana since she worked as a reporter for *The Mystic Messenger.* "Not yet." He picked up the menu and looked it over, trying to decide what to have for dinner. "You hungry?"

"I could eat something. Are you buying?"

"I was hoping you'd pick up the tab," he joked.

With it being a slow night, the bartender brought Dana's glass of wine to the table himself. "Can I get you something from the kitchen?" he asked them.

"I'll have the amaretto chicken salad," Dana said.

"And, I'll have a grilled pork tenderloin and baked potato,"

Nathan added. "Would you bring me another beer with my food too?"

"Sure thing." Scott headed back to the bar where a few other customers had come in and sat down.

"Seriously, anything you could give me about the murder or burglaries would really help me at work."

"It's just my first day. I've barely looked over the case files, but I plan to continue working with the other officers to try and find out who's doing this."

"So, is that your quote for my story?" she asked.

"That's all I can give you until I get more into the investigation."

She took a sip of her wine. "I suppose that will have to do. How do you think you're going to like working at the police department?"

"I think I'm going to like it just fine. It's good to be back home." He took a drink of beer. "Oh, you're not going to believe who I ran into at the hardware store. Aunt Agnes."

"You're kidding. I thought she was in Florida."

"She is, but said she was in town for business. I knew it was her from the sound of her voice." He imitated her high-pitched voice. "Nathaniel?"

Dana laughed. "There's no missing her when she calls your name."

Scott approached their table with their food and Nathan's beer. "Do either of you need anything else?"

Nathan looked at Dana and then back at Scott, "We're fine. Thanks." The bartender walked away.

He knew this wasn't the end of Dana's prodding for information about his investigation, but she let it slide for now. The rest of the evening was small talk about events and politics around town. By seven o'clock, they parted ways, and Nathan headed home to a shower and some sleep.

Chapter Three

Nathan dragged himself through the door of his barren home. The emptiness and quiet gave him a lonely feeling. He walked into the kitchen and got a beer out of the cooler and went into the living room, where he sat in the camping chair. Twisting the cap off of the bottle, he took a long drink of the beer.

He thought about how nice it would be to come home to someone each night. Quickly, he shook that thought out of his head. Been there, done that with Katherine, and that relationship didn't work out. Fortunately, they both realized it, and the split was mutual, parting as friends. *Maybe I could get a dog? I like dogs. Man's best friend.*

He looked around at the hardwood floors and thought the house would be perfect for a dog. He remembered his mother having cats, but they never had a dog while he lived in the house. The long day at work in combination with the food and drink quickly affected him. Fatigue overtook him, and he soon moved to the cot and fell asleep.

The next morning, he awoke before sunrise and slowly sat up. Sleeping on the cot was taking its toll. It felt like every muscle in his body ached. "I sure hope my furniture comes today or I might have to sleep on the floor tonight," he said out loud.

He showered, thankful he remembered to buy soap

and towels over the weekend. Breakfast would have to be eaten in town again, coffee too. He decided to go back to *The Witch's Brew* for that. Growing up, he always got a kick out of the businesses in Mystic trying to steal the tourists from nearby Salem by copying their witching theme. That part of his hometown had not changed a bit.

When Nathan walked into the café, only a few customers sat at tables. He opted to sit at the counter this morning.

Ginger stood behind the counter, waiting for him to sit. As soon as he did so, she filled the coffee cup in front of him. "You look like you need this," she said.

"Thanks. I definitely do." He took a drink of the hot liquid and felt it make its way down, warming him at the same time. "You make very good coffee. Nothing like the swill I drank at the police department yesterday."

"Thanks. That's one thing about owning a café, good coffee will keep the customers coming back."

Nathan laughed, taking another drink.

"Can I get you some breakfast?" she asked.

He picked up the menu and gave it a gaze. "I'll have two eggs, cooked medium, a couple of slices of bacon, and toast."

"Coming right up," she said, turning toward the kitchen.

On the counter, he spotted today's issue of *The Mystic Messenger* and picked it up to see what was happening around town. The first thing he noticed was the byline on the lead story, by Dana Tyler. It told about the city council's decision to sell some of the town's property.

He then moved to the local crime report that included routine traffic tickets, one auto accident, and few drunk-driving arrests. *No major crime wave going on right now*, he thought, except for the Mano Island thefts and murder. He found it a little odd that there wasn't a story about that. Of course, he hadn't given Dana anything on it yet.

One small story did catch his eye, though, and he laughed out loud as he read through it:

A resident became suspicious at 3:49 a.m. when a person

wearing sunglasses, hat, red hoodie, black boots and black gloves was seen standing suspiciously still in the resident's front yard. Police arrived at the scene only to discover that the suspect was a mannequin. According to the police report, "It had been stolen from Martin's Dress Shop and placed in the yard as a joke.

Then, he opened to the inside of the paper and there it was. The one thing he hoped wouldn't happen, an article about him being hired and the photo from his ID card that had just been taken yesterday. Dana had interviewed the chief, and fortunately, that article was small, very vague, and didn't mention his past injuries.

Ginger sat his breakfast in front of him. "Can I get you some more coffee?"

"Absolutely," he answered.

She reached for the coffee pot behind her and filled his cup. "Dana tells me you and her were an item in high school."

"We were." He took a drink of his coffee.

"And then, you left town."

"I enlisted in the army after my parents passed away," he said between bites of bacon and egg.

"Really? My husband, God rest his soul, was an army veteran."

"He must have been a good man."

"He was. He died five years ago. I still miss him every day," she said.

"Were you living here when he died?"

"Yes. He worked at the mattress factory outside of town. I came home from the grocery store on a Saturday and found him napping on the couch. Only he wasn't napping, he'd died in his sleep."

"I'm sorry."

"He had a good life. After his death, I needed something to keep me busy and pay the bills, so I took every bit of our savings and bought this place. I love seeing all of the people here every day."

"And, I bet they enjoy seeing you, too."

"It seems like they do. I heard you were living out at the lighthouse."

"In the house next to it, yes. It was my parents' home where I grew up."

"It's been empty for as long as I've been here. I hope it hasn't deteriorated much." She picked up a towel and wiped the counter next to him.

"A little, but nothing I can't fix. I should get my furniture soon, but what I really need are some curtains. I have no idea what size to get or where to get them." He took another sip of coffee.

"Maybe I could help you with that," she offered. "I decorated my house when we moved here and measured for all of the curtains."

"You'd do that for me?"

"Sure."

"That would be great. I'd pay you for the work, of course."

"You pay for the curtains and I'll charge you ten-dollars over that," she said.

"Ginger, you have a deal." He raised his cup to her.

"Wonderful. When do you want me to come out to measure?"

"I have no idea about my schedule." He stood up. "Suppose you do it when you have time. I had this extra key made this week." He took a key out of his pocket and placed it on the counter, then sat back down.

"You don't mind me being in your house when you're not there?"

Nathan laughed. "I don't mind at all."

"I'll go out there this afternoon when things slow down here. The girls can watch over the café while I'm gone."

He took a final drink of his coffee. "Fantastic. Could you bring me a large coffee to go and my bill?"

"Coming right up." Behind the counter, Ginger picked up a to-go cup, filled it, and sat it in front of Nathan. "You have a good day at work, detective."

"You forgot my bill," he said, taking his wallet out of his rear pocket.

"No charge today," she said.

"I can't do that." He handed her a ten-dollar bill.

"Put your money away. The first meal for a new resident of Mystic is always on the house."

"I appreciate the gesture, but technically this wasn't my first meal here and I'm not really new to Mystic," he said.

"Shut up and go to work before I charge you double," she said, laughing.

"You're the best, Ginger." Nathan started to put the money back in his wallet, but after Ginger turned her back, he slipped it under the plate.

Outside on the street, he saw a newspaper box and picked up an issue since he hadn't finished reading the one inside. He made a mental note to buy a subscription. He then walked the rest of the way to the police department.

Nathan had just finished reading the paper at his desk when his phone rang. "Detective Perry," he said, answering the phone. He listened intently to the dispatcher on the other end of the line. "I understand. Officer McCoy and I will handle it." Nathan scribbled an address on a pad of paper. "Thanks." He hung up the phone and put the note in his pocket.

He noticed the day shift officers were filing by his office on the way to the morning briefing. He fell in behind them, following them to the room. Inside, Nathan found Hank and made his way over. "I need you with me on a call now."

Hank followed Nathan out of the room and to his patrol car. "Dispatch just informed me that there was a burglary last night and someone was injured," Nathan said.

"Where?" Hank asked.

"The newspaper office."

The two men got into Hank's car and left the parking lot.

"What happened?" Hank asked.

"The only information that dispatch had was that the

break-in was at the newspaper office and they found their security officer unconscious on the sidewalk this morning."

When they arrived at the newspaper office, the first thing they noticed was the bloodstain on the sidewalk. Nathan pulled on the glass door, but found it locked. He then saw a man from inside approach the door and unlock it.

"I'm sorry, we're closed today." He acted nervous and started to close the door, but when Nathan held up his badge, the man opened the door and let them inside.

"I'm Detective Perry and this is Officer McCoy."

"Please come in." He opened the door wider for them to enter.

Before Nathan went in, he turned to Hank. "Would you photograph the area and look around for anything that the suspects might have left?"

"Roger," Hank said, starting back to the car to get the camera.

Nathan stepped inside the building. The man that had opened the door locked it again and turned back to Nathan.

"I'm Dan Benson, editor of the paper. Let's go to my office."

Once inside Benson's office, he motioned for Nathan to sit down, but Benson paced behind his desk.

"What can you tell me about the incident?" Nathan asked.

"I'm always the first person that gets here in the morning. It was about four-thirty when I came around the corner of the building and saw Ron lying on the sidewalk." Benson rubbed his forehead.

"What's Ron's last name?"

"Burns, Ron Burns."

Nathan wrote that down in his notebook. "Did he say what happened?"

"No, he was unconscious. I called nine-one-one immediately. I called his wife, but I haven't heard anything."

"Did you notice anyone around when you got to work?"

"No, just that the front door was unlocked. There was blood. He was lying in a lot of blood. Do you think he's going to be okay?"

It was obvious that Benson was a little shaken by what he had seen. "I really have no way of knowing yet. Do you have a security camera?" Nathan asked.

"Yes. We have one inside our lobby. It doesn't cover the outside of the building, but it might show part of the front door from the inside."

"I'd like to get a copy of last night's recording. Could be that the camera might have picked something up."

"Of course. I'll have a copy made for you right now." Benson picked up the phone and punched in three numbers. "John, could you burn last night's footage from the lobby camera onto a disk and bring it to my office right away? Thanks."

"Mr. Benson, have you noticed anything missing?"

"Yes, it's the strangest thing. Our sign that hung above the door is gone. This is what it looked like." Benson handed him an issue of the newspaper. Next to the masthead at the top of the page was a silhouette of an owl. "You do know about the rash of sign thefts in town, don't you?"

"I was just assigned the case and have only briefly read through the case file so far. Has the newspaper received any threats lately?" he asked, placing the paper back on Benson's desk.

"Nothing out of the ordinary. We sometimes write controversial articles, stories about arrests, and the occasional political editorials. We always receive complaints, but none of them have ever been threats."

"Any complaints recently?"

"Nothing I can think of," Benson said. A knock at the door interrupted them and a man walked in. "John, thank you." He took a computer disk from the man, who then left the office.

"Detective, here's last night's footage from the camera."

Another knock from the door and Hank walked in. "I'm

finished outside."

Nathan nodded and looked back at the editor. "Mr. Benson, if you think of anything else please call me." Reaching into his shirt pocket, he realized that he didn't have any business cards yet. He looked over at Hank, who read his mind and handed Benson one of his cards. "You can contact either one of us at that number."

"Thank you, officers."

As they walked out of Benson's office, a female voice called out. "Nathan, wait."

Dana Tyler approached. "Let me walk you out."

Once outside, she looked down at the bloodstained sidewalk and froze. Nathan took her hand and led her a few feet away.

She still stared at the stain as they walked away. "We should get that cleaned up. His blood shouldn't be left there. Everyone will walk by and see it."

"Dana, look at me," Nathan said, and she did as instructed. "Hank will get someone inside to clean the sidewalk."

Hank took the hint and went back inside the newspaper office.

"Are you okay?" Nathan asked. She nodded, but he didn't think she was.

"It's so sad," she said. "Ron should not have gotten hurt over something so meaningless as stealing a sign."

"Unfortunately, it happens all too often."

"But, not in Mystic. Violent crime has never been as bad as it's been lately." She wiped at her eyes.

"The world's changing and those changes are going to happen here too. That's why they hired me. Now, where's that tough journalist I remember from high school?"

She looked up at him and smiled. "The biggest story that tough journalist from high school did was try to figure out who stole sodas from the storage closet." They both laughed. "I should probably get back to work. I'm going to see if Dan will let me cover this story."

"That's my girl."

"If he does, I'm going to need to interview the lead detective." She smiled at Nathan.

"How about that dinner I owe you? Does Friday night sound okay? I should have more details by then."

She thought for a few seconds. "Friday is fine."

"How does six o'clock sound, but you'll have to pick the place. I'm sure all the restaurants have changed since I was last here."

"Bridges is a great place to eat and the tables are fairly private. It's on Chestnut Street," she said.

"That sounds good to me."

"I'll meet you there at six." She stepped closer and hugged him just as Hank walked back out, followed by a janitor with a mop and bucket.

"Don't you dare clean that spot yet," Dana said to the janitor. "We need a picture for tomorrow's paper."

Nathan motioned for Hank and they headed down the sidewalk, leaving Dana arguing with the janitor.

"You sure rekindle things fast," Hank said, once they were out of hearing distance.

"Dana?" Nathan chuckled. "Nah."

They reached the car and got in.

"She's available," Hank said, pulling the car out onto the street.

"I just got out of a relationship and I'm not anxious to get back into one anytime soon."

"Divorced?"

"No, Katherine and I never married. We lived together for a while, but things didn't work out. It was a mutual parting. She had her career in D.C. and I wanted to come back here. We're still in touch. In fact, I need to call her later to see when my furniture will arrive."

"No furniture yet? Where are you sleeping?"

"On a cot last night, but it may be on the floor tonight. My back is killing me. Where are we headed to now?" Nathan asked as Hank stopped the car at a traffic light.

"When I went back inside the newspaper office, the editor received a call saying the security guard had woken up." The light changed to green and Hank proceeded. "I figured we had better get there to question him before his colleagues pounce."

"Good thinking."

A few more blocks down the street, Hank pulled the car into the hospital parking lot.

When they reached Ron Burn's room in ICU, a woman wearing blue scrubs was coming out.

"Is this Ron Burns room?" Nathan asked.

"Yes. I'm Dr. Thomas, and you are?"

"I'm Detective Nathan Perry from the Mystic Police Department," he said, showing his badge. "This is Officer McCoy. Could we talk to you about Ron Burns? We're conducting the investigation into his assault."

"I see," she replied.

"How is Mr. Burns' condition?" Nathan asked.

"He received a large laceration to the back of his head resulting in a concussion, as well as having some broken ribs. He's also covered with scrapes, cuts, and bruises. He's only been awake for a short time and is still pretty groggy from the pain medication."

"Do you think he can answer some questions for us?"

"I'm sure he'll try, but I'm not sure how much he remembers right now. In addition to his head injury, he took a pretty good beating. It could have gone so much worse. It's going to be a long recovery for him." A nurse stepped out of the room and smiled at Nathan as she passed. "You can go in now. His wife is with him, but only stay for a few minutes," the doctor requested.

"Thank you, doctor." Nathan opened the door, and he and Hank stepped inside Around the curtain, he saw Ron Burns laying in the bed, tubes and wires attached to him running to and from machines and monitors. A bandage covered the whole top of his head, and cuts and bruises were visible just about anywhere you could see skin.

The scent lingering in the room reminded Nathan of his own time spent in a hospital. His memory of Afghanistan was like a dream in slow motion, with doctors and nurses moving around trying to talk to him, but him not being able to hear anything. He shook those memories away for now.

"Mrs. Burns, I'm Detective Perry from the Mystic PD and this is Officer Hank McCoy. How's your husband doing?"

The teary-eyed woman looked at her husband and then at Nathan. "The doctor said he'll recover eventually. We just don't know how well he'll recover."

"We'd like to ask him a few questions, if it's alright."

"I'm not sure how much you'll get out of him. They've given him some strong medication." She turned toward her husband and touched his arm. "Ron, honey, the police are here to talk to you."

Slowly, the injured man opened his eyes and looked at Nathan, trying to focus.

"Mr. Burns, I'm Nathan Perry from the police department."

"I'm sorry, my eyes are a little blurry," he said, squinting.

"Ron, they want to ask you about what happened," his wife said.

"Anything you can tell us would be a big help," Nathan said.

Burns tried to wet his lips with his tongue, and his wife gave him a sip of water from a straw. "I heard a noise out front," he said, in slurred speech. "When I got to the lobby, I saw someone on a ladder." He paused to take a breath, cringing with pain. "I thought it was some kids and walked out there to run them off." He paused again. "But, it was two men trying to take our sign off the hinges."

"Two men? Are you sure?" Nathan asked.

Burns nodded his head. "The one on the sidewalk started fighting with me and the one on the ladder must have climbed down because the last thing I remember is being hit on the head." Burns took a deep breath and closed his eyes, opening them again a few seconds later.

"He's very tired," his wife said. "Can't this wait until he feels better?"

"Just one more question. Mr. Burns, can you describe either assailant?"

"I-I can't remember. I'm sorry."

"Thank you, sir. That's all we need for now." Nathan looked at Mrs. Burns. "If he remembers anything else, would you call me?"

Hank handed her one of his cards. "You can reach either of us at this number."

"Certainly. Can I speak to you out in the hall, detective?" she quietly asked.

Nathan nodded, and he and Hank followed Mrs. Burns out into the hallway.

"I probably watch too much television, but is Ron in any danger from the people who did this?" she asked.

"Probably not," Nathan said, but he could read the worry in her eyes. "I'll tell you what I'll do. I can speak with the hospital security department and see if they can make his room a routine stop on their rounds."

"Thank you. I'd really appreciate that," she said and then went back into her husband's room.

Nathan and Hank walked to the elevator, pushed the down button, and waited.

"Has Chief Cabot ever approved police protection for a victim?" Nathan asked.

"We've never had a situation that warranted it and honestly, we really don't have the manpower for it," Hank said, shrugging his shoulders a bit.

The elevator dinged, and when the doors opened, out stepped Dana.

"Are you following me?" Nathan jokingly asked.

"Why yes, yes I am." She laughed.

"I suppose you're here to talk to Ron Burns."

"Yes."

"As a co-worker or as a reporter?" he asked.

She hesitated, thinking for a few seconds. "Both."

"Take it easy on him, Dana. He's in pretty bad shape and his wife isn't doing much better."

"Don't worry, I think I know how to talk to an injured friend." She walked away.

The elevator doors opened again. Nathan just shook his head as he and Hank stepped on board.

"What floor is the Security Department on?" Nathan asked.

"First floor, just off of the lobby," Hank said.

"Good. We'll stop by there on our way out."

"You really think he could still be in danger?"

"I doubt it, but if a guard stops by his room a few times that would be one thing his wife won't have to worry about."

The elevator doors opened to the main floor and Nathan followed Hank to the security office, where they found the head of the department. They explained what happened to Ron Burns and the need for special attention while he was a patient at the hospital. The department manager said he would make sure an officer stopped at Burns' room on each round he made. Satisfied with that, Nathan thanked him.

After the two officers arrived back at the police department, Nathan and Hank went to Nathan's office to view the video footage from the newspaper office. He put the disk into his computer and punched a couple of buttons to watch. They fast-forwarded until they saw some activity.

"There's not much of a view of the outside," Hank said.

"Yeah, mostly just the lobby, but I think we'll still be able to see some of what happened."

"Look, someone's in front of the door," Hank said. "Three-ten a.m."

They continued watching. "There goes the ladder," Nathan said.

"Can you see the guy's face?"

"No, the angle's wrong. Does the department have someone who can pull some screen captures off of this footage and enlarge them?" Nathan asked, pausing the video.

"The I.T. person might be able to do that."

"Might?" Nathan said.

""You have to remember, we haven't had to do anything like this in the past," Hank said. "But, she's pretty good at what she does. When we're finished watching, I'll take it to her."

Nathan started the video running again and watched as the suspects worked to remove the sign.

"Look. There," he pointed at the screen and paused the video again." He put his hand on the wall next to the door." Nathan looked at Hank. "We need to pull those prints. Do we have a crime scene tech?"

Hank sort of snickered. "You've heard of multitasking, right?"

"Yeah."

"Our I.T. tech is also our crime scene technician."

"You're kidding?"

"As far as evidence, she mainly takes photos and pulls fingerprints. For anything more than that, we call the State Police," Hank said.

Nathan started the video again, and both men watched until after they saw Ron Burns assaulted. What little they could see from the lobby camera was still tough to watch. Nathan stopped the video.

"That was brutal." Hank said.

"Yes, it was. I hope they don't show this to Burns until he's recovered."

"Why is that?"

"Seeing yourself in a vulnerable situation can mentally set you back. If you're already in a weakened state, it can do even more harm."

"You sound like the voice of experience," Hank said.

Nathan paused briefly, thinking about his answer. "I

saw a lot of that in Afghanistan." He took the disk out of his computer and got up. He and Hank were heading out the office door just as Gloria rushed in, nearly knocking them down. "Sorry, Hank." She looked at Nathan. "I didn't think you'd ever get back."

"Why? What's the emergency?"

"What? Oh no, no emergency. I just wanted to give you my report." She handed him a small stack of papers.

"Your report on what?"

"Businesses that have had their signage stolen recently."

"There's so many!" Nathan gazed at the page she had given him. "This is excellent work, Gloria. Nice job. Thank you."

"That's what I'm here for." She was beaming as she turned and left.

Hank led Nathan down to the basement and to the Evidence Room. Inside they found a dark-haired female behind a counter.

"This is Mallory Duncan, our evidence and I.T. technician. Mallory this is our new detective, Nathan Perry."

"It's nice to meet you." She extended her hand.

Nathan shook hands. "It's good to meet you too. I have a feeling we'll be crossing paths a lot in this job."

"What can I do for you, detective?" she asked.

"There was an assault and theft at the newspaper office this morning." He handed her the computer disk. "This is security footage from last night. The camera is in the lobby of the office, but some of the assault was captured on it. Can you see if you can blow up and print a photo of the perpetrator's face?"

"I'll see what I can do," she said.

"When you look at it, you'll also see that he put his hand on the stone wall next to the door. I'd like for you to go down there as soon as possible to try and get a print off the wall."

"I'll get right on that. Anything else?"

"Make sure you log the disk as evidence," Nathan said.

"I'll do that." She pulled out a log sheet and had Nathan sign it.

"He also needs some business cards," Hank said. "Mallory handles that too."

"A jack of all trades."

She just smiled. "I'll get all the info to you as soon as I can."

"Thanks." The two officers went back upstairs.

"If you don't need anything else, I need to get on patrol," Hank said.

"Sure. Go ahead. Thanks." Hank left and Nathan went back to his office. At his desk, he looked over all of the information Gloria had collected about the thefts and began making notes. His cell phone rang. He looked at the caller ID and then answered. "Hello."

"Hi, Nathan. I hope I caught you at a good time."

"Your timing is perfect. How are you, Katherine?"

"I'm fine. Are you getting settled in with hometown life again?"

"Well, somewhat. I could even more, if I had my furniture. Do you know when it'll arrive?" he asked.

"That's actually what I'm calling about. It should be there tomorrow. I gave the movers your cell phone number and they'll call you when they get to town."

"Thanks." He took in a deep breath and slowly let it out. After becoming uncomfortable with the silence, he asked, "How's work at the new location?"

"Oh, same as always. I'm getting used to the new surroundings. Other than not having your furniture with you, how are things with you?"

"Actually, pretty good. I'm working on a case where someone was murdered during a break-in that happened not long before they hired me and just last night someone was assaulted during a burglary," he said.

"That's terrible. Any suspects?"

"That's the problem, everyone's a suspect because no

one's a suspect."

"Sounds like you have your work cut out for you."

"My job depends on making an arrest for the burglaries and the murder, but that's my problem." He wanted to change the subject. "Say, you should come visit for the weekend. My house is right on the ocean, you'd love it."

"You know I can't," she paused. "It would be a step backwards for us and it wouldn't work."

He leaned back in his chair. "Yeah. I guess you're right. You were always right, which is why I miss you. I'll let you know when my stuff arrives. I love you, Katherine."

She laughed. "Love you, too."

He started laughing with her. "Goodbye." He hung up his cell phone still laughing. Their relationship had always been a special one, and even though they were no longer in love, they still had a special love for one another.

His thoughts then shifted back to his case. Picking up the phone, he dialed Mallory's extension.

"Mallory Duncan, can I help you?"

"It's Nathan. Can you tell me how to look up any other crimes that happened on the same nights as the Mano Island burglaries?"

She guided him through the steps to finding the information on the computer. "Thanks. I think I found what I need."

At the end of the day, Nathan gathered his things to head home. Gloria popped around the corner of his door. "Ginger Raines stopped by and said to give this to you." She handed him a sheet of paper with measurements on it.

"Thanks, Gloria. She measured my windows for curtains today."

"You better get some up soon, or all the single ladies in town will be camped outside your house waiting to enjoy the view."

He laughed. "Exactly why I'm getting curtains. Thanks."

That night was the Mano Island Homeowners Association

meeting. Nathan always enjoyed the drive along the highway to the island. With the sun low, the sky had an orange glow over the ocean, more beautiful than any sunsets he had seen anywhere else in the world. As he drove out to the island, his thoughts were on what he planned to say to the members of the association.

He pulled into the parking lot of the Community Center, a building that could easily pass for a college auditorium. He parked between a Jaguar and a Lexus. He looked at the expensive cars. "Definitely above my pay grade," he mumbled and walked into the building.

At the front of the room was a man conducting the meeting in the packed room. Nathan assumed it was Quentin Mahoney, the HOA president. "We've had some complaints lately that a few residents are not mowing their grass to the proper height and also using grass blowers during quiet hours. Those owners will receive a written warning from the Association first, but if it continues, then a fine will have to be administered."

"Quentin, we can't help it if the lawn company we hire works late," one man said.

"Jim, you'll just have to speak with them about seeing to our lawns here on the island before their other customers," Mahoney replied.

Nathan chuckled to himself. How do these people live with all the crazy rules?

"I see that Detective Perry from the police department has come in. I think we've covered everything on the agenda and I'd like to turn the meeting over to him," Mahoney said.

The audience turned and watched Nathan make his way up the center aisle to the front of the room. With all eyes upon him, he felt like he was walking to the electric chair. He shook hands with Mahoney and waited to be introduced.

"For those of you that don't know him, this is Detective Nathan Perry from the Mystic Police Department and he's here to speak with us about the rash of burglaries that we've had here on the island." Mahoney then took a seat to the side.

Most of the group clapped their hands in what Nathan thought was an underwhelming welcome. "Thank you. As Mr. Mahoney said, I'm here to speak a little about the burglaries, but mostly about how to avoid future break-ins."

He looked out over the room, which he estimated to contain about one hundred people. He recognized a few faces from newspaper photos about their entrepreneurial successes or their donations to some of Mystic's charitable organizations.

As he continued his gaze, he spotted a familiar face. Dana sat in the second row. He nodded to her and she smiled back.

"Whoever has been doing these burglaries is mainly hitting homes without alarm systems or video surveillance cameras. We've been asking to view the security video from those of you that do have security systems so we can see if anything might have been caught on your video feeds from your neighbors' break-ins. If we haven't contacted you yet, please call the police department and leave a message. Someone will be back in touch about viewing your recording."

"Do you have any leads on the perps?" someone asked. Chuckles from the audience followed the question.

Nathan tried not to laugh at the comment from the person who likely watched too many television police shows. "I really can't talk about specifics of the case, but we are looking into some leads that we have."

"You said we. Aren't you the only detective with the police department? And aren't you probably working on other cases as well?" another man asked.

"Yes sir, I am the only detective, and yes, I have other cases, but I can assure you that this one is my priority at this time. I also have the whole Mystic Police Department at my disposal and we are all involved in solving this."

"What about Raymond Miller's murder? What's being

done about that?" someone asked.

"Again, I can't really talk about an ongoing investigation, but we are checking every lead. That's why it's so importation to view as many surveillance videos we can."

"You said earlier that you came here to talk to us about avoiding future break-ins. Can you speak to us about that?" a very well-dressed lady from the back row asked. Mumbles throughout the crowd sounded in agreement with her question.

A man from the other side of the room stood up. "It seems to me that more police patrols out here would be a big step."

"Yes, sir, that would help. Mystic isn't a large city, yet we still have a good size area to cover. The police department has twenty-five officers, which includes sergeants, lieutenants, the chief, and myself. I know that sounds like a lot, but we have three shifts per day, seven days a week, to serve over forty thousand people. Everyone wants more patrols in their neighborhoods, but we can't increase patrols for everyone. I agree that more police presence could deter the burglaries, but who's to say if we did that here on the island that break-ins wouldn't increase somewhere else?"

No one responded to that question.

"If I may, I'd like to make a recommendation on something that your Association might consider."

"Please, go on. We'd like to hear what you have to say," Mahoney said from his seat.

"I would suggest that you consider having your own security department for the island. Possibly even making this a gated community for your own protection."

"Who would pay for that? Would the city chip in?" someone asked.

"I can't speak for the city, but some communities I'm familiar with around the Washington, D.C. area where I used to live increased the fees for their associations to help pay for it."

Grumbles from the crowd grew and he knew acceptance of that idea would be voted down right away.

"There may be other ways to come up with the money to pay for a security patrol. All I am doing is making a suggestion. Meanwhile, the department will continue to work toward finding the person or persons who are responsible for the burglaries and murder. Thank you for allowing me to speak with you today."

Mahoney stood next to Nathan and the audience applauded, somewhat better this time than when he began. Mahoney adjourned the meeting, and everyone headed to the refreshment tables.

Nathan tried to make his way through the crowd to Dana, who had already headed for the back exit. So many people wanted to talk to him, but he wanted to catch up to Dana first. "I promise to come right back in, but I need to speak to someone before they leave," he said.

He made it outside just before she reached her car. "Dana, wait."

"Good talk in there. You had them wrapped around your finger until you mentioned paying for security," she said.

"Yeah, and they all want me back in there for an encore in a few minutes. We're still on for dinner Friday night, right?"

"Yes, we are. I'm not letting you out of that so easy." She smiled and got into her car and drove off, leaving Nathan on his own for another hour of questions and answers over refreshments.

Chapter Four

The following morning, Nathan came in the back door of the police department and headed down the hall to his office. Just as he reached his door, he heard Gloria call his name.

"Nathan. I thought you'd never get here," she said, coming out of the breakroom.

He looked at his watch. "It's only five after eight."

"There was another burglary last night on Mano Island."

Hank had now joined them as they walked to Nathan's office. "Another one?" he asked.

"Yes, while everyone was at the Association meeting," she said.

"Oh, that's not good at all. I need coffee for this." Nathan grabbed his cup from his desk and went to the break room with Gloria and Hank following.

"That's not all," Gloria added.

"There's more?"

"Yes, but we better go back to your office for the rest."

He and Hank both got coffee, and the three of them went back to Nathan's office and sat down.

"Here's the officer's report." She handed a file to him. "The owner's dog was injured."

"Damn." Nathan looked through the file and took a drink of coffee.

"What happened?" Hank asked.

"The report says when the owner and his wife returned from the Homeowners Association meeting, they found the house had been broken into and their Labrador unconscious," Nathan said.

"They thought she was dead," Gloria said.

"How's the dog now?" Hank asked.

"The report doesn't say."

"I called the vet this morning and the dog had been stabbed, but will be okay," Gloria said.

"Thanks. Would you tell Officer---" he looked at the report, "---Avery that I'd like to see him when he comes in?"

"I will. He'll be in for the afternoon shift. If there's nothing else, I need to get back to the front desk."

"I think that's all. Thanks."

She got up and left the room. Nathan read more on the report.

"This is interesting. The report says along with stuff from the house, one of the items stolen was a boat motor. They broke into their boat storage building that's on the water behind the house."

"What else was taken?" Hank asked.

"The usual stuff, computer, jewelry, cameras."

"I wonder if they knew there was a dog in there, or if they were surprised by it?"

"My guess would be surprised, otherwise they probably wouldn't have selected that house," Nathan said.

Someone at the door cleared their throat and the two officers looked up and found Chief Cabot standing there. "Gentlemen."

"Chief, come in," Nathan said.

The chief sat down. "I just heard there was another break-in on Mano Island last night."

"Yes, sir. I just received the report." Nathan held up the file.

"I also understand that it happened while you were

speaking to the Homeowners Association."

"Yes, sir. That's correct."

"Did you know the mayor lives next door to that residence?"

"No, sir. I didn't realize the mayor lived on Mano Island."

"He just called and he's not happy. It could easily have been his home."

"Well sir, I would advise the mayor to think about getting a security system, if he doesn't already have one," Nathan said.

The chief's face began to turn red as he stared at Nathan. "Is it true that you suggested to the Homeowners Association that they hire their own security?"

"Yes, sir."

"So, that's your solution to the burglaries, for them to them to take care of the problem themselves? Detective, I didn't hire you to advise people to get their own security." The chief stood. "I hired you to solve the damn crime! The mayor suggested I fire you immediately and I considered doing just that, but I've decided to give you another chance. I'm giving you one week to get a handle on this and I expect a report on my desk by next Wednesday. Understood?"

"I understand. Thank you, sir."

The chief turned and left.

"Wow," Hank said. "Only your third day on the job and he's already threatened to fire you. I think you set the new record."

Nathan let out a deep breath. "I thought for a minute I was going to have to pack my things up and head back to D.C. today."

"He usually blows up at someone at least once a week. Everyone can breathe a little easier now that you're the winner for this week."

"He really thinks I can solve this in a week? We need to figure out these burglaries. We're missing something."

"I have to get out on patrol. Anything in particular that

you want me to do to help?" Hank asked.

"As a matter of fact, there is. Can you add Mano Island to your regular patrol? That would give them an extra officer out there and I'll see if we can get another night shift officer out there too. Maybe the visibility of an extra patrol will get the mayor off the chief's ass and in turn off mine."

"Sure, I can do that, but you better clear that with Lieutenant Matthews, so he'll know why I'm not on my regular route."

"I'll do that. Thanks."

Hank left for his patrol, and after Nathan sent an email to Lieutenant Matthews, he pulled the files for all of the burglaries. He tried laying everything out on his desk, but it was too small, so he decided to move to the break room where the tables were larger. He had only been working in there for about twenty minutes when an officer walked in.

"Detective Perry?"

"Yes."

"I'm Ryan Avery. I regularly patrol Mano Island. Officer Wheeler said you wanted to speak to me."

"Yes, I did." Nathan got up and shook hands with the young officer. "Would you like coffee or a soda?"

"No, thank you."

Nathan stepped over to the soda machine and dropped some coins to get himself a drink. He took it back to the table and sat down. "Please sit down. I've been studying the past burglaries and also your report on the one last night."

Officer Avery sat down. "What can I do to help?"

"I saw where the home of the recent burglary sits on the ocean and his boat was in the building?"

"Yes, sir. His boat was dry-docked in the boathouse for the winter and the outboard motor was stolen."

"I think I'll take a drive out there tomorrow and look around myself. Are you working tomorrow?" he asked.

"Yes, sir. I'm on the day shift tomorrow. Would you like me to go with you?"

"No, I think I'll go myself first."

"Just let me know if you need anything, detective." Officer Avery got up.

"Please, just call me Nathan."

"Yes, sir. Nathan." He turned and left the room.

Nathan started gathering the files and putting them back together when his cell phone rang. "Hello."

"Is this Nathan Perry?" the voice on the phone asked.

"Yes, it is."

"Mr. Perry, this is Chuck Murray from Over the Road Movers. We are just entering Mystic and have your furniture to deliver."

"That's great. Do you need directions to my home?"

"I have the address punched into our GPS, so I think I can find it. I wanted to make sure someone would be there to let us in."

"I'm at work right now, but I can meet you there in about fifteen minutes. The house is on the ocean and there's a lighthouse behind the main house. You shouldn't have any trouble recognizing it."

"We'll meet you there."

"Thanks." Nathan took the files and put them in his briefcase and then went up to the front counter. "Gloria, my furniture is arriving and I'm going to head on home to unlock the house. I'm going to finish working on these cases at home. You can reach me on my cell phone, if I'm needed for anything."

"I'll make a note of it and will let dispatch know also."

"Thanks. See you tomorrow."

Nathan headed down the hallway and out to his truck to drive home.

After the movers took everything inside and put the furniture in place, it felt a little more like home to him. Since he and Katherine had lived together, they both had furniture and his small amount didn't nearly fill up the house. But at least he now had a bed and knew he would sleep better tonight.

The next morning, four inches of snow greeted Nathan when he walked out of his house to go to work. Instead of parking in back, he parked his truck on the street in front of the police department where it had already been cleared of snow. He climbed the six steps to the front door two at a time and went inside.

He found a different officer manning the front desk, a young male. "Good morning, Detective Perry."

"Good morning, George. Where's Gloria?"

"It's her day off."

"I see. Do you know if Officer Avery is here?"

"Yes sir, he is. I believe I saw him in the break room with some of the other officers before the briefing starts."

"Thanks." Nathan headed down the hallway. He reached his office almost at the same time as Officer Avery rounded the corner.

"Good timing, Ryan. Come in, I need to talk to you," Nathan said, unlocking his door.

Both men sat and Nathan pulled a file folder out of his briefcase and opened it on his desk. "The report that you filled out on the most recent burglary shows several expensive things taken. What did the owner have to say about what was stolen?"

"Not much. When I got there, Mr. Wright already had the list of the stolen items written out," Avery said.

"Could be they're so used to the burglaries that they know what we'll need when we investigate."

"I suppose so, but he was pretty anxious to know how long before he got a police report to turn in to his insurance company."

"That is interesting. How well do you know Mr. Wright?"

"I know him when I see him. He always waves when he's outside and I drive by on my patrol, and he owns the Apple Harvest Orchard west of town."

"I wonder how business is at the orchard?" Nathan

asked.

"Not too well, especially this year. I understand that the really warm and dry weather we had last spring caused a decrease in apple production," Avery said.

"One bad year could really hurt a business like that, wouldn't you think?"

"Probably so."

"Thanks, Ryan. I think I need to go buy some apples. Is the orchard open this time of year?" Nathan asked.

"Yes, sir. They're open year-round and sell fresh produce that's shipped in from warmer climates. Would you like me to come with you?"

"No, this is purely an unofficial visit, but thanks."

Officer Avery left, and shortly afterward, Nathan drove out to the Apple Harvest Orchard. With the highway being slightly snow-covered, traffic was light. Reaching the orchard, he had no problem with finding a parking spot in the nearly empty lot. He found the sidewalk from the parking lot had already been cleared of snow, and he followed it to the orchard's main building.

Once inside, he walked down the right aisle, first making his way through all the bins of vegetables where he found mushrooms, lettuce, kale, various herbs, radishes, and parsnips. Down the second aisle, he found the apples, taking note of the price.

"Can I help you with something?" a young girl asked.

"I'm just looking for now. Thanks. Oh, these apples are more expensive than usual, aren't they?"

"We had a bad summer. We have shopping carts over there if you need one," she suggested, before leaving to help another customer.

Nathan did pick up a small bag of Gala apples and a gallon of cider to take home. Just as he started toward the checkout, someone called to him from behind. "Excuse me, aren't you Detective Perry?"

He turned around and saw an older man walking toward

him. "Yes, I am."

"I thought so. I recognized you from the HOA meeting. I'm Henry Wright, owner of this place."

"It's nice to meet you. I'm afraid I have my hands full," Nathan said.

"Let me help you." Wright took the bag of apples from Nathan, and they shook hands. Both men started walking toward the front of the barn-like building.

"My house was broken into and my wife's dog was nearly killed. I've yet to get a copy of the report for my insurance company so I can file my claim," he said.

"Yes sir, I was just looking at the list of stolen items this morning. Was that outboard motor attached to your boat?" Nathan asked.

"No, no it wasn't. I had it in the boathouse for the winter."

"Where was the boat?"

"I had it on dry-dock in the boathouse also. When do you think I'll get a copy of the report?"

They reached the checkout and Nathan paid for his purchase. "I'd like to come out and look at the boathouse, if that's okay?"

"Your officer has already looked at it. What's the purpose?"

"Well sir, different officers have worked the different burglaries out on Mano Island and I think if one set of eyes can look around each crime scene for similarities, it could make solving the crimes go faster."

"I don't know. I'll be here until late in this evening," Wright said.

"I could come out tomorrow and probably bring a copy of the report for your insurance company with me," Nathan prodded.

"Well, I suppose if you have to look it over, I can get away from here for a little while. What time will you be there?"

"How does three o'clock sound?"

"That would be fine. I'll meet you at my house tomorrow

at three. Oh, and don't forget that report."

"I won't." Nathan took his purchases, left the building, and headed back to town.

Back at his office, he printed out the report that Mr. Wright wanted for his insurance company and placed it on his desk. His computer dinged, indicating he had received an email. It was from Lieutenant Matthews, giving his approval for the extra patrol on Mano Island.

Lastly, before leaving for lunch, he looked through the phone messages that were on his desk. One of the messages was from Dana. He picked up the phone and called her back.

"Hi Dana, it's Nathan. I'm returning your call."

"I wanted to let you know that I might be a little late for dinner tonight. I have an interview set up with someone for a story due tomorrow and will have to finish it first."

"I have an idea. Instead of going to a restaurant, why don't you come to my house and I'll fix dinner for us. My furniture was delivered yesterday and I bought a refrigerator. If you're a little late, that's okay."

"That's a great idea. I'll be as quick as I can though."

"Is there anything special you want for dinner?"

"No, anything will be fine, but nothing too heavy since it may be late."

"Great. I'll see you some time after six."

"I'll bring the wine. Red or white."

"I'm not sure. Bring some red, I guess." Nathan hung up the phone.

After lunch, he spent the afternoon going through the cases that Lieutenant Matthews had given him upon his arrival and wrote a report up on each one.

Before heading home at the end of the day, he took the copy of Wright's police report and put it in Officer Avery's mail slot with a note about his visit tomorrow. On the way home, Nathan stopped by the supermarket and picked up a few things for the dinner with Dana.

At his house, he tossed his keys on the kitchen counter,

sat down the bags of groceries, got a frosted mug from the freezer, and poured himself a beer. He then began preparing a pot of potato soup.

An hour and a half later, he heard his doorbell ring and went to the door to answer it.

"I'm sorry I'm late." Dana stepped inside, shaking snow onto the floor. She removed her coat, scarf, and gloves, hanging them on a hook by the door. "The snow has started again."

"I have just the thing for a cold night. How does potato soup sound?"

"That sounds wonderful, but that's not something light to eat." She followed him into the kitchen.

"Yeah, sorry about that, but it's so cold, I thought it would be okay."

"It's fine and I'm sorry, I forgot to stop and get wine."

"No problem. How about a beer?"

"That would be great."

He retrieved a frosty mug from the freezer for Dana and poured her beer. "Are you ready to eat?"

"I am. Can I help with anything?"

"I have everything ready. You could get the bread out of the oven while I get the bowls for the soup."

"The house looks really great with your furniture in it, except for all the boxes sitting around," she teased.

"Thanks. It'll take me awhile to unpack them and I still need to get some pictures for the walls, but it's nice having a bed instead of a cot to sleep on." He ladled hot soup into a couple of bowls and took them to the dining room table. Dana carried the loaf of French bread on a platter and sat it on the table too.

Nathan went back to get a couple more beers and some butter. They sat down to eat. "This is delicious. I'm impressed. Where did you learn to cook?"

"When you live alone, you learn to survive."

After their meal, they moved to the living room and

Nathan lit a fire in the fireplace. When he stood up, he moaned and grabbed his back.

"Are you okay?"

"Sleeping on that cot was probably a stupid thing to do. I should have bought an air mattress instead. I'm not as young as I used to be, you know," he joked.

"Come here and sit next to me." She patted the couch cushion next to her.

He sat and she started giving him a neck massage. "Your muscles are really tight. You need to relax."

"That feels really good." He closed his eyes and let her work his muscles.

After only a few minutes, Nathan turned and grabbed her by the arm, swinging her around and landing her on his lap. He wasted no time pulling her to him and kissing her. She wrapped her arms around him and returned the kiss.

"I know this isn't what you had in mind when you came out here tonight, but would you like to continue this in the bedroom?" he asked.

"How do you know this isn't what I had in mind?" She smiled and stood, still holding onto his hand.

Nathan stood and led her to his bedroom.

The next morning, he woke up and reached to the other side of the bed, finding it empty. He heard noise coming from the kitchen and smelled bacon. He got up, pulled on a pair of sweatpants and a t-shirt, and, after taking care of business in the bathroom, he walked into the kitchen where he found Dana making breakfast.

"Good morning," she said. "I hope you have time for breakfast. I made scrambled eggs and bacon."

"That sounds good." He got a cup from the cabinet and poured himself some coffee. The clock on the wall showed seven-thirty. "I need to be at work by eight-thirty," he said.

"Breakfast is ready." She brought two plates of food to the small table in the kitchen and sat down to eat.

Nathan walked over to the table, forgetting to hide his

limp.

"Why are you limping?" she asked.

Damn it, he thought. "I suppose now is as good of a time as any to tell you."

"What are you talking about?"

"When I was in Afghanistan, I was injured from an IED explosion."

"Oh my God, Nathan. Are you alright?"

"I am now. I had been sent to a nearby town to investigate some thefts from the base. The vehicle I traveled in hit the IED. I suffered an injury to my eardrum and a fractured leg."

"I had no idea."

"I lost the hearing in one ear for a while. It took several surgeries on my ear and one on my leg to get me back to as close to normal as I am now."

"Does your hearing or your leg injury hamper your work?"

"No, the doctors cleared me for this job and I also passed the physical the chief sent me to do. I mostly have the limp when I first get up in the morning. Dana, I don't want anyone else knowing what happened, at least not yet. I have to make sure everyone knows that I can do this job before they know about my injuries."

"I won't say anything."

"I appreciate that." He started eating.

"What do you have planned for today?" she asked.

"Oh, a little of this, a little of that."

"Nathan, I'm not asking as a reporter, but as the woman you shared your bed with last night."

"I'm sorry." He swallowed. "Talking to the woman I shared my bed with and not to the reporter that I shared my bed with, I'm going out to Mano Island today and look around." He took another bite of food.

"That's interesting. What do you hope to find?"

"I don't know. That's why I'm going out there."

"Okay, we need to set some ground rules here," she said.

Nathan stopped chewing and looked up at Dana.

"When I'm with you, unless I'm acting in my official capacity as a reporter, I will not print anything you say unless you tell me it's okay."

"Really?"

"Really."

"Well, you should know that I'm in my official capacity as a police officer twenty-four-seven and it will take me some time to get used to being more comfortable talking about work with you." He stood and took his plate to the sink. "I've got to get in the shower, but you go ahead and finish. Stay as long as you want."

"Go take your shower." She threw a kitchen towel at him.

Nathan quickly shaved, showered, and dressed casually for the day. He came back out and saw Dana still at the table drinking coffee and reading the newspaper.

"I hope you don't mind. Your newspaper was delivered and I wanted to read it."

"No problem. Thanks for breakfast. I'm sorry I have to rush off."

"I'll do the dishes and then I'll be out of here."

"Thanks. Will you lock the door when you leave?" he asked, putting on his coat.

"Of course."

"Dana, about last night."

"Hey, I had a great time, but I know you aren't looking for a relationship. Neither am I. Now go, you're going to be late."

He smiled, glad that she understood. After giving her a quick kiss on the lips, he left. Driving into town, he felt he and Dana might just have the perfect friendship.

What is it they call it? Friends with benefits? Yeah, that was it.

Chapter Five

Nathan was only fifteen minutes late when he walked into the office after leaving Dana at his home that morning. He set the box of framed certificates and photos that he brought with him on the edge of his desk.

Logging onto his email, he found the ballistic report on the Miller murder from the State Police. After reading and printing it, he placed it into the file. He started going through his box, trying to figure out where to hang the framed items when his phone rang. "Detective Perry."

"Nathan," Gloria said. "The county coroner's been waiting for you."

"Sorry, I was late. Could you send him back to my office?"

"Certainly."

Nathan hung up the phone and moved the box from his desk to the floor.

A knock announced the coroner's arrival. "Detective Perry, I'm Vince Scanlon."

"Mr. Scanlon, it's nice to meet you." The men shook hands. "Have a seat."

"Thank you, Detective."

"Please call me Nathan."

"Nathan, I've brought the autopsy report on Raymond Miller." He handed him a set of typed papers. "I didn't actually do the autopsy myself since I'm only a funeral director. The

State Medical Examiner's office in Boston does the autopsies and they sent the report to me."

Nathan studied the report. "One gunshot wound to the chest. I received the ballistics report just this morning. It showed he was shot with a forty-five caliber weapon."

"Mr. Miller bled out on his kitchen floor. I'm only speculating of course, but I believe if he could have gotten help right away, he might have lived."

"The whole thing is a damn shame." Nathan closed the file and placed it on the desk.

"Mystic used to be such a nice, quiet town," Scanlon said. "It still is, I suppose, but it seems that more crime is moving our way every summer from the city. It's not good for the town at all."

"What funeral home do you work at?" Nathan asked.

"I'm at Davidson's."

"What happened to Mr. Cowen? He was the director there when I used to live here."

"He retired and moved to Florida with his wife several years ago. I read in the newspaper that you're originally from Mystic. I guess a lot has changed since you were here last."

"It has. More businesses, more hotels, and from what I read on the Visitor's Bureau web site, Mystic is even getting some small conventions."

"We're growing fast. Unfortunately, it's not all for the better."

"Excuse me," Hank appeared at the doorway with another man. "Hello Vince, if I can interrupt for a minute. Nathan, there's someone here you need to meet."

"I should probably be going anyway," Scanlon said.

"Wait, Vince. You should meet him too," Hank said. He and another gentleman stepped into the room. "This is Sam Denzinger, homicide detective with the Massachusetts State Police. Sam, this is Vince Scanlon, our coroner, and Nathan Perry, Mystic P.D.'s new detective."

"How do you do, gentlemen?" Denzinger shook their

hands. "I didn't mean to interrupt your conversation."

"No, that's fine. Vince just brought over the autopsy on the Mano Island murder," Nathan said.

"That being said, it's a pleasure meeting you, Detective Denzinger, but I do need to get back to the funeral home," Scanlon said. "Nathan, if you need anything, you know where to find me."

"Thank you, Vince."

Scanlon left. "Gentlemen, please sit down," Nathan said.

"I have to get back on patrol, but I'm sure there's things you two need to talk about," Hank said, stepping out of the office.

Denzinger took a seat in front of the desk. "Well, I sure know how to clear a room, don't I?"

"I've been known to do the same thing at times."

With a little gray around the temples, probably from his police experience, Denzinger was older than Nathan by about five years. "Let me explain why I'm here," Denzinger began.

"You mean this isn't just a social call?"

"I wish it were. Chief Cabot called me to help investigate the Mano Island murder."

Nathan's eyes widened and he straightened up in his chair a little. "He did, did he?"

"I can see by your reaction that you didn't know."

"No, I didn't, but that's okay. I welcome your assistance. I just wish that he would have told me he had called you." In truth, Nathan was worried about the Chief calling in the State Police. It could be an indicator on whether he got this job on a permanent basis.

"Look, I'm not here to take over the investigation," Denzinger said. "I'm here to let you know that I'm available to assist, should you need it. As far as I'm concerned, it's your case."

"I appreciate that." Nathan pushed the file on the desk toward him. "Here's what we have so far and it includes the autopsy and ballistics reports that I received this morning."

Denzinger took his time looking through the file and then handed it back to Nathan. "The break-ins are occurring about every ten days."

"Yes, they are."

"If they stick to that schedule, the next one should be within the next week."

"We're going to increase patrols out on the island during that week. Mostly in unmarked cars so not to be so noticeable."

"It sounds like you've got things under control. I'm not sure why the Chief thought you needed help."

"There is something you might be able to do for me."

"I'll be glad to do what I can."

"I'm guessing the stolen items are probably being fenced in Boston. Do you think you could check on anything that might have turned up there?"

"I can certainly do that. Do you have a copy of the list of items?" Denzinger asked.

"I can email you a copy of the whole file."

Denzinger handed Nathan his card.

"I'm afraid I don't have any cards yet." Nathan scribbled his name, number, and email address on a piece of paper and handed it to Denzinger.

Denzinger stood. "I'll be in touch if I come up with anything on the stolen items."

"Thanks."

"You know, I live over in Salem. We should get together for a drink some time. I'd like to know more about your background."

"I'd like to hear about your background too." The two men shook hands and Denzinger left. If first impressions meant anything, Nathan liked him and thought they could work very well together.

Before heading out to meet Henry Wright on Mano Island, Nathan spent the rest of the day working more on the cases that Lieutenant Matthews had given him. He had unsubstantiated most of them, but there were a few that he actually felt needed further investigation.

At three-o'clock on the dot, Nathan parked his car in Henry Wright's circular driveway. Pulling in right behind him was Officer Avery.

"Hello, Ryan. I'm glad you could join me. Did you remember the report for Mr. Wright?"

"Yes, sir. I'll get it from my car."

"Wait, leave it there for now. How well do you know Wright?" Nathan asked.

"I've known him since I was a kid."

"He seems pretty anxious to get the insurance report. Do you think that's strange for him?"

"Actually, no I don't. Mr. Wright is pretty tight when it comes to money and since the orchard didn't do well last year, I'd say he needs the money."

"Good. I was afraid he was trying to defraud the insurance company."

"I really don't think that's the case with him," Avery said.

Wright came out of the front door to greet him. "Good afternoon, detective. The boathouse is out back. If you'd like to see it, please come with me." He led them through a gate and around the house into the backyard.

"Mr. Wright, do you remember Officer Avery?"

"Yes, I do. Good afternoon."

"Good afternoon, sir," Avery said.

Mr. Wright's backyard opened to the ocean. Attached to the boathouse was a private dock.

"Here's where they broke into the building." Wright opened the door so Nathan could examine the damage to the frame.

"It certainly looks like someone took a crowbar to it." Nathan took a picture of it with his phone, and then they walked inside the building. "Nice boat."

"It's a thirty-footer," Wright said.

Nathan looked at the large garage door that opened up

to the water. "It seems that they could have opened that big door and pulled the boat right out."

"That door has both a padlock and a deadbolt on it. Even if they could have gotten past those locks, they would have then had to know the code for the door opener and then spend the time putting the motor back on the boat," Wright said.

"Is that the only security you have down there?"

"I'm afraid so."

"What about security cameras around the house?" Nathan asked.

"No, nothing. I always intended on installing a system for the house, but never got around to it. I guess I waited too long."

"Where did they enter your house?" Nathan asked.

"The backdoor window was broken and then they could reach the lock." Wright took him over to the door where a wooden board was now where the window used to be.

Nathan took a photo of the door. "How's your dog?"

"He'll be fine and probably home tomorrow."

Nathan and the two men walked back to the front of Wright's house. Just then, three cars drove past them and turned into the driveway several houses down the street.

"That's Charlene Miller returning home. She's been staying out of town with family," Wright said.

"Charlene Miller?" Nathan asked.

"Her husband was the victim of the murder," Officer Avery explained.

Nathan turned to Officer Avery. "Ryan, did you bring the report that Mr. Wright needs for his insurance company?"

"Yes, sir. It's in my car. I'll get it." Avery fetched the report and handed it to Nathan, who passed it on to Mr. Wright.

"Thank you so much. Is there anything else you need Detective Perry?" Wright asked.

"No. I think we're finished here. Thank you."

Wright went back inside his house, leaving the men

outside by their cars.

"What do you think, detective?" Officer Avery asked.

"I think this was done by the same people that have burglarized the other homes."

"You know there's a pattern in the break-ins," Avery said.

"I do. Every ten days or so," Nathan said.

"What are we going to do?"

"What would you do, Ryan?"

"Well, we can't really do a stakeout because we don't know where they'll hit next. I suppose we need to warn everyone out here."

"That could cause a panic and we don't really want that. How about extra patrols out here for a while?"

"I could sure use the help."

"I've already contacted Lieutenant Matthews and he's approved it."

"Thank you, sir."

Nathan gave Avery a nod and both got into their cars. Nathan drove back toward the mainland and Avery continued his patrol of the island.

Just after he crossed the bridge leaving the island, Nathan's cell phone rang. "Detective Perry."

"Nathan, it's Gloria. I have some information you need before you get back to the office." She spoke quietly, almost in a whisper.

He could hear enough of the background to tell she was calling from her desk. "What is it, Gloria?"

"Joe Cassidy just left the chief's office."

"Joe Cassidy?"

"He's a local private investigator. He told me the Homeowners Association hired him to investigate the burglaries out on the island. He had an appointment with the chief and I'm sure it was to tell him he's been hired to investigate."

Nathan stopped his car at a red light. "Why do you think that?"

"After Cassidy left the building, the chief called to tell me that he wanted to see you as soon as you got back here and he was not using his happy voice."

Laughing. "I didn't know the chief had a happy voice." The traffic light turned green and Nathan proceeded through the intersection. "I just left Mano Island and will be at the department after I get something to eat. I skipped lunch."

"I'll let the chief know."

"Thanks, Gloria." Nathan decided to stop by *The Witches Brew* when he saw Hank's car parked on the street. He parked his own car and walked in, spotting Hank sitting by the window. They exchanged waves and Nathan joined him at the booth. "How was your day?"

"It's a typical Monday." Hank took a drink of his coffee and swallowed. "Yours?"

"It's a cold Massachusetts morning. Enough said."

Hank laughed and Ginger approached the table, setting a cup of steaming coffee in front of Nathan.

"You look like you could use this,' she said.

"You read my mind. Could I have a BLT and an order of your famous onion rings?"

"Coming right up, handsome." She turned and headed to the kitchen, laughing the whole way.

Nathan took a sip of his coffee. "What are you doing after you're finished here?" he asked Hank.

"I'm patrolling until six."

"Good. I want to go down to Church Street to see where those sign thefts occurred. Want to come with me?"

"Sure. It beats driving around all afternoon."

"Why do you think someone would steal signs from businesses? I mean there's no monetary value to them, right?" Nathan asked.

"That's what has all of us baffled. Some of them were antique or at least unique in some way, but not all of them. We figured it was a bunch of kids, but haven't found any of the signs yet.

"If it had been kids, you'd think they would have dumped them somewhere to keep their parents from finding them?" Nathan asked.

"You'd think."

"Were any caught on camera?"

"Of the businesses that had security cameras, they only had them inside of the businesses to catch shoplifters. We checked and nothing outside was caught on camera."

"What else is on Church Street?"

"The part of the street where the thefts took place is a pedestrian mall. No vehicle traffic at all. There's some restaurants, souvenir stores, a couple places that do tours of the town, a bank, and the Baptist Church," Hank said.

Nathan popped up. "Does the bank have an ATM?"

"Right on the street for the tourists to use."

"ATM's have cameras. How close were the thefts to the bank?"

Hank thought for a second. "Two were across the street. Three are on the same side as the bank and the other two are down the street and probably out of range for any camera."

"We need to speak to the bank manager about getting a copy of that video from the nights of the thefts."

"The bank is open late tonight, so someone should be there to talk to," Hank said.

The two officers finished eating. "I'll follow you down to Church Street," he told Hank. Once they arrived, the two officers took a walk down the street and came to the Mystic Ice Cream Shoppe first.

"They've already put up a new sign," Hank said.

The sign now hanging above the door showed a smiling witch holding an ice cream cone.

"When were they hit?" Nathan asked.

Hank checked his notebook while Nathan took a picture of the new sign. "October fourth and they were the first theft."

"Is this new sign the same as the old one?"

"I think it is."

. Nathan looked across the street. Down the block a little, he saw the bank and their ATM. "Where's the next closest business that was hit?"

"That would be the Church Street Deli." Hank pointed to the deli two stores down.

"The ATM camera might not have gotten this one, but it sure should have recorded someone taking the deli sign," Nathan said. "Let's go talk to the manager."

The men crossed the street and entered the bank. "Hi, Linda, this is Nathan Perry, our new detective at the PD."

"Hello, Mr. Perry. Would you like to open an account with us?" she said with a wink.

"Maybe soon, but not today."

"Linda, who is the manager here at the bank now?" Hank asked again.

"Oh, that would be Bobby, I mean Robert Kent."

"We'd like to see Mr. Kent, please," Nathan requested.

"Sure."

She picked up the phone and called the manager. He appeared immediately. Dressed in a tailored black suit and tie, he appeared to be a very fit forty-year old.

"Officers, how can I help you?" Mr. Kent asked.

"Mr. Kent, I'm Officer McCoy and this is Detective Perry." The men shook hands.

"Could we speak to you in your office?' Nathan asked.

"Certainly, right this way." Nathan and Hank followed the manager to his office and sat down once inside. "Now, what did I do to earn a visit from the local police?"

"There have been a series of thefts on this street in the past few months and we believe your ATM camera may have caught one or more of them," Nathan said. "We'd like to obtain a copy of your camera footage to see."

Kent rubbed his chin, where it looked like he was trying to grow a Van Dyke. "I'm afraid I can't do that."

"Why?" Hank asked.

"I have to look out for the bank's customers and the

tourists that use that machine. Their privacy is a concern for the bank."

"You do realize that we can get a warrant for your recordings?" Nathan asked.

"Yes, detective. I do understand and with a warrant that releases the bank from any responsibility. How far back do you need it?"

"The first theft was October fourth."

"That's three months ago. It'll be close to see if the company still has the recordings that far back. Most ATM recordings are only kept for thirty days. Once you have your warrant, you'll have to check with the off-site company that's responsible for the cameras and see what they still have," Kent said.

"What's the name of the company?' Hank asked.

"Commonwealth Security in Boston. Now, if there's nothing else, I do have a lot of work to do."

"Could you at least contact the company to tell them to get the recording ready? It might save some time," Nathan asked.

"Of course."

Nathan and Hank thanked the bank manager and then left. Back out on the sidewalk, they discussed what just occurred.

"He wasn't very cooperative, was he?" Hank said.

"No, he wasn't."

"What do you make of that?"

"I think he's looking out for himself and not wanting to get into trouble with the main office or the depositors. I suspect he's just covering his ass," Nathan said, but other thoughts raced through his mind.

"You'd think he'd want to be cooperative with the police department though.

The two men started across the street to the Church Street Deli. They stopped in front of it.

"Who's the District Attorney?" Nathan asked.

"Daniel Grant," Hank said. "He's been in that position for several years. He's good at it too."

"How hard will it be to get a warrant for the videos?"

"I don't think it'll be a problem. You need to meet him anyway. You'll probably be working with him often."

While they stood in front of the business, a gentleman walked outside to talk to them. "Gentlemen, I'm Tom Stuart. I own this deli, could I have a word with you?"

"Certainly, Mr. Stuart. I'm Detective Perry and this is Officer McCoy. What can we do for you?"

"Can we go inside?" The men went inside the deli and took a seat at an empty booth. "It's about my sign getting stolen. I filed a police report, but haven't heard anything about what's being done."

"You're in luck, Mr. Stuart. Detective Perry was hired this week and one of the cases he was assigned is the sign thefts," Hank said.

Stuart looked at Nathan, apparently waiting to hear some news.

"As a matter of fact, that is why we're down here today," Nathan said. "I wanted to get a look at the street where the thefts occurred and see the layout. We have some ideas and hopefully we'll be able to update all of the business owners soon." Nathan knew it was a line of nonsense, but thought it would satisfy the store owner.

"What kind of leads do you have? Do you have a suspect?" Stuart asked.

"We really can't go into specifics at this time, but rest assured that we're working on the case."

Stuart paused before saying anything else, as if he was taking in all of Nathan's words. "Okay. What do you need from me?"

"Do you have any idea who would want to steal your sign?" Nathan asked.

"I just figured it was a bunch of kids doing it for the fun of it. You don't think so?"

"It's a possibility, but we're not limiting ourselves to just that scenario. Your sign had a witch on it, like the others, correct?"

"Yes. Yes, it did and I'm still waiting for my insurance money before getting another one made, but am also a little hesitant to take the chance on it getting stolen too."

"I don't blame you there, Mr. Stuart. Have you had any customers that showed a particular interest in the sign?" Nathan asked.

Stuart appeared to be thinking for a bit. "No, I can't think of anyone. I just can't believe anyone from here would do this."

"Thank you, Mr. Stuart. I'll see that you get a copy of the police report right away. I'm sure that's what the delay is with your insurance company," Nathan said.

"I'll be waiting for it." Stuart stood and walked away to speak to some other customers and Nathan and Hank left.

They continued their walk down the street. Their final stop was at the Mystic Chamber of Commerce, the location of the last theft. They entered the building and found two men standing in the lobby talking.

"Mr. Forrester." Hank said.

"Yes. What can I do for you, Officer?"

"I'm Officer McCoy and this is Detective Perry. We'd like to talk to you about the recent theft of your sign."

"Well, it's about time. We can talk in the library. Please follow me. John, you come too," he said to the man he had been talking with.

Once inside the Chamber's library, Forrester closed the door. "Now, what is going on with these thefts?"

"Detective Perry, this is Benjamin Forrester. He's the president of the Chamber of Commerce," Hank said.

"Mr. Forrester, we're here to continue with the investigation into the thefts of the signs from the businesses on Church Street. What can you tell me about it?" Nathan asked.

"What's there to say? Our sign was stolen."

"Yes, sir. Do you remember anyone hanging around for a prolonged period that day? Someone that normally wouldn't?"

"We have tourists in and out of here all day. I don't remember anyone specific," he said.

"It's the middle of January. How many tourists would you have in here during that time?" Nathan asked.

"More than you would think."

Nathan took a deep breath. "I saw a security camera in the lobby. Have you checked it to see if it may have caught the theft occurring?"

"I don't need to check it. I know nothing's on it," Forrester said.

"And, how do you know that?"

"That camera's been broken for about six months."

"Did any of the other businesses' cameras catch anything?" the other gentleman asked.

"I'm sorry. I didn't get your name," Nathan said.

"I'm John Hawkins, the City Clerk."

"Well sir, I'm afraid at this time that information is for the police only. Mr. Forrester, thank you for your help."

"You don't have any clues, do you? You're just going through the motions to satisfy the business owners. It figures Paul Cabot would hire someone that doesn't know what they're doing.

Nathan turned to Forrester. "If you think of anything, please call me at the police department." Nathan left the room and Hank followed him out onto the street.

As they walked back to their cars, Nathan expressed his opinion. "I don't like that man."

"Which one?" Hank asked.

He thought for a second before answering. "Both."

The men laughed.

"Forrester is just a little too arrogant for my taste and Hawkins, well I just didn't like him at all." They reached their cars. "Thanks for coming with me today. I'm still trying to get acclimated back to the town."

"Anytime. That ate up a good amount of my patrol time this afternoon and helped make the day go faster. I've got a few hours left, so I better get going."

The two men got into their cars. Hank headed toward the harbor area and Nathan went south to the police department. He parked in his usual spot and went inside, heading to the front desk to check in with Gloria and found her dealing with a well-dressed elderly woman with bluish-colored hair and bright red lipstick. He checked his slot for messages while she dealt with the lady.

"Mrs. Carson, the police department simply cannot spare a patrolman every night to sit in front of your home to keep the kids from hitting your house with eggs."

"I don't understand why not. I pay taxes. Why shouldn't you be able to help me?" She clutched her purse in front of her. "I'm a friend of Chief Cabot's, you know. I may just have to take this up with him."

Nathan couldn't help but snicker and he was pretty sure Gloria heard him.

"I didn't say we couldn't help you. I'll ask the shift sergeant if he can increase patrols on your street at night," Gloria offered.

"Well, I suppose that might help, but if something isn't done, I'll have to take matters into my own hands."

"Now don't be doing that, Mrs. Carson. Let us handle it."

"We'll see." The little lady turned and left the building.

Nathan pulled a chair up next to Gloria and sat down. "Do you think you convinced her?"

"I hope so. I bet she'll be watching out her window all night to count how many times a patrol car goes by. I'm even tempted to drive by myself just to satisfy her."

Nathan laughed. The more he got to know Gloria, the more he admired her. "Is the chief in?"

"He is and he's waiting for you. He's been calling me

about every thirty minutes asking if you were back yet."

"Well, I'm back and on my way up to see him." He stood and moved the chair back to where he got it.

"Good luck," Gloria uttered.

Nathan patted Gloria on the shoulder and walked to Chief Cabot's office. Taking two steps at a time, he reached the second floor quickly, but stopped to steady himself at the top. His leg nearly gave out when he landed that last step. Too much, too quick, he thought.

He stepped around the corner and knocked at the chief's door. "Gloria said you wanted to see me."

"Ah yes, Detective Perry, please come in and close the door behind you." Chief Cabot, bifocals on, sat behind his desk that had files strewn all over it.

Nathan closed the door, thinking that couldn't be a good sign, and sat down. "What can I do for you, sir?"

He leaned back into his chair. "I had a visitor this morning. Do you know Joe Cassidy?"

"No, the name doesn't ring a bell." He hated lying, but he didn't want to get Gloria into trouble with the chief.

"He's a local private investigator and the Homeowner's Association hired him to find out who is doing the burglaries on Mano Island. Do you know who recommended they hire a P.I.?"

"No, sir."

"The mayor suggested it because he doesn't have faith that you can solve it."

"Did the mayor specifically say that?"

The chief hesitated before answering. "No. I'm speculating because he wasn't too happy after he heard that you told the association to hire their own private security."

Nathan shifted in his chair. "I didn't tell them to specifically do that. I may, however, have suggested that hiring private security was an option."

"Did you suggest any other options?"

"I told them they might consider making the island a

gated community."

"Regardless, Mr. Cassidy came here today to ask to see the case file and offer his assistance with the case."

"What did you tell him?"

"I told him that concerned citizens were not given access to case files for ongoing investigations."

"Thank you for saying that. I agree," Nathan said.

"But, that doesn't mean that Mayor Newcomb won't order me to give him access. So, where are we in the investigation?"

"I'm afraid not very far. No fingerprints were found at the Miller home, but I did get the autopsy and ballistics reports. I can email them to you. Other than knowing it was a forty-five caliber that killed him, there's not much to go on right now. I am going to go see the murder victim's wife tomorrow. She's been out of town and returned today."

"What about identifying the gun that did the shooting?"

"I've turned that over to the State Police, but with their backlog, it could take a while."

"Very well. Keep me updated, detective."

"Yes, sir."

Nathan left the chief's office and went to his own. Sitting down behind his desk, he went through the messages he had picked up earlier. One of them was from Joe Cassidy. Since he didn't get anywhere with Chief Cabot, Cassidy probably thought he'd give Nathan a try. "Fat chance," Nathan said out loud.

Another message was from the Mystic fire chief requesting his assistance on an arson case. Nathan separated the messages into three piles, call now, call later, and call never. Joe Cassidy's message was the first one in the call never pile, which he pushed off his desk and into the trash can.

It took Nathan the rest of the day to return the immediate calls, including a long conversation with the fire chief. By the time he was finished, it was late, and he was more than ready to go home.

Chapter Six

"Detective Perry?" the timid voice at his office door said.

"Hello, Mallory. Please come in," he answered, after swallowing his gulp of coffee. It was the only way he could get through the cold early mornings like this.

"I have the report from the state police crime scene unit about the murder scene."

"Thank you." Nathan looked through the file, which also included photos of the murder scene.

"I received video from the home security system across the road. I'll be viewing it as soon as I get back to my office."

Nathan looked up from the file. "Thank you. Let me know if it shows anything useful. What about the newspaper office scene? Were you able to get any prints from the outside wall?"

"I was able to get a palm print, but it was a rough surface. I only got a partial fingerprint. It's been sent to the state police for a match, but it could take a while to get the results. I'm not sure it'll even be enough to get a hit."

"We'll just have to wait and see. Let me know what you find on the video."

"I will. Oh, I almost forgot." She handed him a small white box. "Here are your business cards. I had them put a rush on it."

"You have no idea how much I have needed these."

"Just call if you need anything else and I'll let you know after I view the video." She left the office.

Nathan put the file on his desk and opened the box of cards. He liked the design and put a few of the cards in his badge holder. He then picked up the Friday issue of the newspaper that he brought into work that morning.

The main story, with Dana's byline, was about Ron Burns and the newspaper office burglary. She had quotes from the editor and from Mrs. Burns, but none from him. The only reference to the police investigation was that the police department was in the early stages of the investigation.

Dana did add that Ron Burns did not remember anything about his assault. "Good girl." The one thing it included that Nathan didn't know was that Burns was home from the hospital.

Nathan opened a different file folder from his desk and thumbed through a few pages, until he found what he was looking for and dialed a number on the phone.

"Hello."

"Mrs. Burns? This is Detective Perry from the police department. We met at the hospital."

"Yes, I remember."

"I was wondering if your husband would be up for a visit today?"

"When would you be here?" she asked.

"I'd like to come over now, if I could."

"I suppose that would be okay. He just finished breakfast."

"Thank you. I'll see you in a little bit."

He picked up the case file for the Burns assault and stepped out of his office, locking the door behind him, and went down to the front desk. "Gloria, I'm going to question Ron Burns. He's home from the hospital."

She motioned him closer and he leaned down. "I don't suppose I could go with you? I'd love to do some field work."

"I was hoping to take you with me when I visit Mrs.

Miller, the murder victim's wife. I could use your help more with that visit. I think she might respond better to a woman."

She smiled. "I suppose you're right. That visit will need a woman's touch. Just let me know when you go."

"I will. I won't be gone long." He turned and left. He could tell she was disappointed that he didn't take her with him, but she was right; the Miller visit will need a woman along.

When he arrived at the Burns' residence, Mrs. Burns greeted him. "Hello, Detective Perry. Please come in. Ron is in the living room."

He entered the home, noticing a wheelchair by the door. "How is he doing?"

"He's better, but still has a lot of pain."

They entered the living room where Burns was sitting with a walker within his reach.

"Ron, this is Detective Perry. He visited you at the hospital."

"You certainly look better than you did the last time I saw you," Nathan said.

"Thank you. I'm sorry, I don't remember you," Burns spoke slowly.

"I understand. I'm investigating your assault at the newspaper office. How are you doing now that you're home?"

"I feel better just being here, but still in a lot of pain. Between a concussion and some broken ribs, I'm not moving too quickly yet."

"I've had both a concussion and broken ribs. They can be very painful. I was hoping you might remember something from your attack. Anything at all might be a help to the investigation."

"I wish I could help, detective, but I don't remember anything about it."

"Could you look at a couple photos?" Nathan showed him the blurry photos from the newspaper office's surveillance video. "Do you recognize these men?"

Burns put on a pair of glasses and took the photos from Nathan. His wife moved over behind him to look also. He looked at the photos for a long time. "I don't recognize them. I'm sorry."

"Are they the ones that attacked him?" his wife asked.

"We believe so."

"Mr. Burns, if you remember anything, would you call me at the police department?"

"Yes, I will. Thank you." He handed the photos back to Nathan.

"I'll walk you out." His wife led Nathan to the front door. "We really appreciate the work you're doing to find the men who did this to Ron. I'm pretty sure he won't be going back to work after this."

"What will he do?"

"He's worked long enough to retire from the newspaper."

"It's good that he has that option. I'll keep you updated on anything new that we find."

"Thank you."

Nathan drove back to the department, and he went to the radio room. "Melinda, do I have any messages?"

"A few and the chief wants to see you. He wasn't in a very good mood either."

"I wonder what I did now. Thanks." He looked through the messages as he headed down the hallway to his office. With none of them being urgent, he unlocked his door and placed them on his desk before walking up the stairs to the second floor to see Chief Cabot. He rounded the corner and stood at the door where he found Mayor Newcomb sitting with the chief.

"Detective Perry, come in," the chief said.

"I'm sorry, sir. I was told you wanted to see me, but if you're busy with the mayor, I can come back later."

"Detective," the mayor said. "You're the reason I'm here. Come in and sit down."

Now, he really wondered what he had done. He took the

chair next to the mayor and awaited his demise. After all, why else would the mayor take the time to come see him?

"Detective, are you any closer to solving the burglaries and murder on Mano Island?" the mayor asked.

"Sir, with all due respect, I was only just assigned this case a week ago. It normally takes more time than that to get familiar with a case."

"I suppose in a bigger department you would have more officers to assist you?"

"That's correct. Officer McCoy is assisting, but there's only so much two officers can do."

"Are you saying you need another person to help with the case?" the chief asked.

"Well, sir, that wouldn't hurt." Nathan was hoping that the chief would assign Gloria to help full-time with the case.

"I think we can get you some assistance, detective," the mayor said. "Do you know Joe Cassidy? He's a local private detective."

He couldn't believe what he just heard. "Chief Cabot mentioned him to me, but he's a private citizen."

"I understand your concern, but he's from here and I believe his assistance could be a valued asset."

"Again sir, with all due respect, I'm from here also."

"The difference being that you have been away for seven years," the mayor pointed out.

Before Nathan could protest more, the chief interrupted. "Detective Perry will be happy to work with Joe, won't you, Detective Perry?"

He knew he was defeated. "Yes, sir. I will be happy to work with Mr. Cassidy."

"Excellent," the mayor said. "I'll tell Joe to contact you about the case."

Nathan looked at the chief. "If there's nothing else, I need to go see the District Attorney about a warrant."

"Of course, we're finished here."

Nodding to the mayor, Nathan stood and left.

By the afternoon, Nathan felt like he'd been put through the paces after the meeting with the chief and Mayor Newcomb, and the day wasn't over yet. He parked his police car in the courthouse parking lot and went inside, searching for the District Attorney's office.

Finding it at the end of the hallway, he opened the door and stepped in.

The secretary looked up. "Can I help you?"

"I'm Nathan Perry, Mystic police detective. I need to see Mr. Grant about a warrant."

"Please have a seat and I'll tell him you're here."

Nathan took a seat. He hated waiting. It reminded him of all the doctor appointments he waited for after getting home from Afghanistan. He picked up a magazine and began flipping through the pages.

"Detective Perry?" A well-dressed man stood at the hallway entrance. With brown hair and brown eyes, he looked like he could be on the cover of GQ magazine.

"Yes." Nathan stood.

"I'm Daniel Grant." The two men shook hands. "It's nice to meet you. Please come in."

Nathan followed him to his office. "Please sit down. Chief Cabot tells me you were in the Army."

"Yes, eight years."

I was in Army for four and I'm still in the Reserves. Did you serve in the Middle East?"

"Two and a half years in Afghanistan with the Criminal Investigative Command."

"Excellent. I was in Kuwait for almost two years."

"Both tough places," Nathan said.

"I agree. We'll have to have lunch sometime soon and exchange war stories. But, I understand you're here today about a warrant."

"Yes. I'm working on the sign thefts and I'm hoping the bank's ATM camera on Church Street might have caught something. The bank wants a warrant before they'll release the video. I have the Probable Cause Affidavit already filled out." He handed the form to Grant.

The attorney looked over the form. "This looks in order. I'll talk to Judge Mason as soon as I can, but I doubt there will be any problem getting this."

"Thank you. Can you call me at the police department when you get it?" He placed one of his cards on Grant's desk.

"I will. You're also working on the Mano Island cases too, aren't you?"

"Yes, I am."

"How is that going? I live on Mano Island, so I have a personal interest, as well as professional, in this case. I also knew Raymond Miller."

"I won't lie. It's not going as well as I hoped. There wasn't a lot of evidence collected prior to me being hired, but from looking at the case reports, I think the perpetrators may be coming in by boat. They've also done their homework."

"How so?"

"The only homes that were hit were without security systems."

"Most of the homeowners I know use the same security company," Grant said. "Have you checked that angle?"

"I'm going to have Officer Avery canvass the residents out there during his regular patrol to get that information."

"Good. If there's anything I can do, please let me know."

Nathan stood and extended his hand. "I will. It was nice meeting you and I look forward to us working together."

Grant also stood and shook Nathan's hand. "I think you'll be a real asset to the police department and to the town."

"Thank you."

Nathan left the courthouse and walked back to his car. He liked Daniel Grant and would have to remember to ask Dana more about him.

Later that night, Nathan turned his pickup truck into the parking lot of *Bridges Restaurant* to meet Dana and do the interview for the newspaper. The first thing he noticed when he walked in was how dark it was inside. However, the room was exactly as Dana had described it, with tall backings on the booths for added privacy.

"Table for one?" the hostess asked.

"No. I'm meeting Dana Tyler for dinner," he said.

"Miss Tyler? Oh yes, she's already arrived. Please follow me."

The dimness of the restaurant added to the calming effect, as well as the black and red color theme.

Finally reaching the table next to the huge fireplace, Nathan saw Dana, who had been hidden by the booth.

"Good evening," he said. He leaned down to kiss her on the cheek and then slid into the booth opposite side of Dana.

"Would you like a cocktail, sir?" the hostess asked as she placed a menu in front of Nathan.

He saw Dana had a glass of white wine. "Bring a bottle of what Miss Tyler is having."

"Very good. I'll have your server bring it right over." The hostess turned and walked away.

"It seems like I remember this being the Benton's home when I was a kid," he said.

"Yes, it was. When Mr. Benton died, the family sold it to a company that converted it into this. The food is wonderful too."

Nathan browsed the menu. The waiter approached the table and showed him the bottle of wine before filling his glass. He took a sip and nodded his approval.

"Are you ready to order?" the waiter asked.

Dana ordered the shrimp alfredo, and Nathan requested the pan-fried halibut.

After the waiter left, Nathan took another drink of his wine. "Aren't you going to ask me any questions for the interview?"

"I thought we could enjoy dinner first," she replied.

"I'd rather get it out of the way and then enjoy dinner and the company." He tipped his glass to her.

"If you insist." She took a small notebook and a pen from her purse and began. "The theft of the signs appears to have escalated to an assault now. Why do you think that happened?"

"I don't think they realized the newspaper office had security on duty. He probably surprised them, causing a scuffle."

"They?" she interrupted. "You think there were more than one?"

"The security camera at your office caught two people removing the sign and then assaulting Mr. Burns. It wasn't pretty."

"Have you identified them?"

"Not yet."

"What happens next with the case?"

He took a drink of his wine. "We're following up on some leads and before you ask, no I can't elaborate on what those leads are."

"I understand. I don't like it, but I understand. What about the previous thefts, is there anything you can tell me about those?"

"We think those burglaries were likely done by the same people. We have to consider all the evidence from each location and put it all together."

"What evidence do you have?"

"Again, I can't really say right now, but I'm confident that we'll find the people. One thing I would like for you to mention in your article is that Ron Burns isn't able to identify his assailants."

"Sure, but why is that so important?"

"When I visited him at the hospital, his wife was worried that whoever injured him might think he could identify them and come back to finish the job."

"Do you think that's possible?"

"Not really, but for their peace of mind, it would be good for them to read that."

"I'll make sure to include it." She scribbled some notes down. "Can you tell me anything about the thefts and murder on Mano Island? How is that investigation progressing?"

"Since I'm new to the police department, I'm still familiarizing myself with the files. I'm working on it every day though."

"Do you think there is connection between the Mano Island burglaries and the sign thefts?"

"I doubt it. The things that were stolen on Mano Island are high price items, not something like the signs. Although, as I discovered from the insurance claims, some of those signs were worth a lot of money."

She added to her notes. "Nathan, my editor is really anxious to get an article in the newspaper with more about you coming back to Mystic. It wouldn't be many questions."

"I don't know, Dana. I'm not too keen on people knowing about my personal life. You've already written that I got the job at the PD. What more do you want?"

"Maybe more in depth about why you decided to leave Washington, D.C. and return to Mystic," she said.

At that moment, the waiter stepped up to the table with their food.

"This looks delicious," Dana commented to the server.

"Will there be anything else?

"I think we're fine. Thank you," Nathan said, and the server left. "I met Daniel Grant today." He took a bite of his fish.

"He's done a great job prosecuting cases."

"Hank pretty much said the same thing. I'm glad to hear someone else say it."

Just as Dana was about to take a bite of her pasta, someone approached the table.

"Nathan? Nathan Perry? I thought that was you." Standing next to their table was a slender, short man dressed in a somewhat wrinkled gray suit.

Nathan could not figure out who this man was until

Dana spoke. "Joe, how are you? Nathan, you remember Joe Cassidy from high school."

"Of course. It's been a long time." Thankful that Dana recognized his lapse in memory, he shook hands with Joe.

"Say, did Chief Cabot tell you I've been hired by the Homeowners Association to investigate the murder and break-ins?"

"He did."

"I'd like to come by your office to discuss the cases with you. I'm sure the chief told you the mayor said I could see the files."

"Yes. Call me tomorrow and we can set something up."

"Fantastic." Joe turned to Dana. "You look as lovely as always." He touched her hand on the table and Nathan noticed her cringe, if only slightly.

"Joe, we're kind of on a date here," Nathan said, taking Dana's other hand.

"Of course, I'm sorry. I should have known you two would rekindle that spark you had back in high school. I'll call you tomorrow, Nathan." He turned and left.

"Thanks for saying we're on a date. He's always complimenting me in a creepy way like that." She shuddered.

"You mean we aren't getting back together? I'm heartbroken." Nathan held his hands over his heart and then laughed.

"As far as Joe Cassidy is concerned, we are."

"Here, here." Nathan raised his glass of wine and so did Dana in a toast to each other.

The waiter stopped at their table. "Would either of you like to order dessert?"

"Not for me, but I would like some coffee," Dana replied.

"Nothing for me. Thanks."

After Dana had finished her coffee and Nathan paid the bill, they walked to her car. "Dinner was lovely and thank you for answering my questions for the newspaper," she said.

"I'm happy to help, when I can."

She unlocked her car. "I guess I should be getting home."

Nathan took her hands into his and leaned down to kiss her. He stepped back when he broke off the kiss. "We did tell Joe we were on a date," he whispered.

Dana laughed. "Goodnight, boyfriend."

"Goodnight, girlfriend." He waited until she drove off before he got into his truck and headed home himself.

****

Nathan woke with a start on Saturday morning after hearing a loud thump from his kitchen. Someone was in his house.

He slowly slipped out of bed and picked up his gun from the table next to the bed. Opening the door carefully, he was thankful that he had oiled the hinges last week to silence the squeak.

Stepping lightly down the hallway, he held his gun at eye level pointed down the hallway. Whoever had been in the kitchen was now in the living room.

He swung around the corner, holding his gun on the intruder.

"Good morning, Nathan. Nice boxers."

"Ginger, what the hell are you doing in my house?" He lowered his gun and slowly released the hammer.

"You wanted me to hang your curtains. It was slow at the café this morning, so I thought I'd come do that now. You gave me a key the other day, remember? Since you were sleeping, I started in here. Guess I woke you anyway, eh? Sorry."

"It's fine."

"You know we don't really know each other that well yet. Don't you think you should put some pants on?" she asked.

Nathan looked down, forgetting he was still wearing his boxers. Feeling embarrassed, he turned and went back to the bedroom and put on a pair of sweatpants and a shirt.

When he returned, he found Ginger standing on a chair hanging the first curtain for the front window. With Ginger not being a petite woman, he was a little worried about her steadiness on the chair. "Be careful, you could fall." He rushed over to stand next to her.

"I'll be fine. Oh, I almost forgot, I brought you some biscuits with gravy and a large coffee from the café. If you want it, you better get it while it's still hot." She stepped down and moved the chair to hang the next curtain.

Nathan took the opportunity to get the food and quickly came back into the living room. He sat his coffee on the table by the couch and held the foam insulated container with the biscuits and gravy and ate while standing next to Ginger again. "Thank you for bringing breakfast. It's really good."

"Since you're a bachelor, I figured you could use a good breakfast. I also noticed that your kitchen is a mess."

Nathan swallowed and then stepped over to get a drink of coffee. "Yeah, I guess I need to hire a housekeeper."

"I'm glad you said that. How about hiring me to clean your house?"

"When would you have time with having the café to run?" He took another bite of his breakfast.

"Friday afternoons are pretty slow right now. I could clean here and then it would be all ready for any weekend guests you might have."

Nathan thought about it while taking another bite of his food. "What makes you think I'll have weekend guests?"

"Let's see, there was the look you kept getting from Dana the last time you both were in for lunch and the fact that I saw a coffee cup in your sink with her shade of lipstick on it."

Nathan looked at Ginger, raising one eyebrow. "You're very observant."

She finished hanging the curtains and stepped down from the chair. "Am I hired, or not?"

Nathan laughed as he walked to the couch and sat down to finish his breakfast. "If we can agree on a fair wage, it would be great to have you clean my house."

"Good. I can start right now." She picked up the chair and started carrying it into the kitchen.

"We haven't even agreed on how much I'll pay you yet." He got up and followed her.

"Oh, you'll be fair." She started opening and closing cabinet and closet doors. "Don't you have any cleaning supplies?"

"I've only bought a broom so far," he said from the kitchen table.

"I can't clean a house without supplies." She stood staring at him.

He finally took the hint, got up and went to the bedroom. Coming back with his wallet, he handed her two twenty-dollar bills. "Will this be enough to get what you need?"

"It's a start." She took the money. "I'll start you an account at Driscoll's Hardware. They'll send you a bill at the end of each month and I'll check with you first for any big purchases." She moved the chair over to the sliding glass doors to start hanging the curtain there.

Nathan thought for a few seconds. "Wait. Let's go to Driscoll's now. You can get the supplies you need and I'll get a step ladder so you won't be climbing on the chairs."

"You're going to be a good boss," she teased.

Nathan smiled as he went to the bedroom to change clothes.

Monday morning

Dana Tyler, carrying her large cup of coffee, arrived a little late for work. After hanging up her coat, she sat at her desk, took a drink of coffee, and started her computer.

A young intern approached Dana's desk. "Miss Tyler, Mr. Benson wanted to see you as soon as you got in."

"Thanks, Cindy." Dana started reading her e-mail and noticed the intern still standing next to the desk. "Is there something else?"

"He was pretty adamant that you come right away."

"Sounds like he's not in a good mood."

"Yes, ma'am. I think you're right."

She smiled at the girl. "Well, it wouldn't be Monday morning, if he wasn't in a bad mood."

Dana stood and followed the intern to Benson's office. Cindy sat at her desk outside the editor's door and Dana walked in. "You wanted to see me, Danny?"

Benson looked up from his computer. "Yes, please close the door and sit down."

Dana turned to close the door and then sat in the chair in front of the desk.

"I read the story you submitted over the weekend about Detective Perry. I honestly expected you to dig deeper into his past. Find out what he's done since he left Mystic, since he left the Army."

"That's what I wrote about. I can't help it that he led a boring life all those years."

Benson laughed. "Word around the office is that you and he were an item back in high school and that maybe you've rekindled that flame now that he's back. Could be because of that you failed to include some things about him that happened when he served in Afghanistan. Am I close?"

Dana shifted in her seat, but tried to keep her anger hidden. "I haven't rekindled anything, but a friendship. What did you find out about Afghanistan?"

"As if you don't know, but I'll play along. Your Detective Perry was injured in an IED explosion over there and spent a lot of time in the hospital when he returned to the States. He lost his hearing and suffered a serious fracture of his thighbone. It wouldn't surprise me if he isn't physically qualified for the police department." He pointed his finger at Dana. "That's the story I want to print and I want you to write it."

"How did you find out about his injuries?" she asked.

"Oh, so you do know about it."

"He told me last week, but asked that I not write about it.

Chief Cabot knows about it too, his hearing has returned, and he passed his physical with the police department. There's no reason for people to question his ability, but if it shows up in the newspaper, they will. He just wants to do his job and I told him I wouldn't include it in the story."

Benson pursed his lip and nodded. "I understand. Don't worry about it." He dismissed her from his office with a brush of his hand in the air.

Chapter Seven

Early Monday morning, Nathan stepped out of his truck in the rear parking lot of the police department and pulled his coat collar up around his neck as he walked to the back entrance of the building. Once inside, he removed his gloves, putting them in his pocket, and blew his warm breath onto his hands.

When he reached his office, he hung up his coat and picked up his coffee cup. Normally, he would have stopped on his way to work to get his coffee at Ginger's, but today he didn't want to be out in the cold any more than he had to.

The break room was filled with officers waiting for the morning briefing. Most of them acknowledged him when he passed by. Everyone in the department had been very welcoming after his hiring, and he was pleased that they accepted him into the brotherhood.

Finally making it to the coffee pot, he filled his cup. As usual, it wasn't as good as the coffee at *The Witch's Brew*, but at least it was hot.

"Ladies and gentlemen, the briefing will start in five minutes," Sergeant Donnelly called from the doorway. "Please make your way into the room."

Nathan hadn't been to a morning briefing since his first day; he wasn't required to attend, but decided to join them today. He was the last one to enter the room and stood in the back.

Sergeant Donnelly read over the previous weekend's activity, which included a water main break. "The Street Department will be working on Decker Street today to repair the break. Traffic will still be routed onto Temple Street and then back onto Decker past the break via Olympic Avenue. Obviously, due to the snow and cold temperature, the streets are slick, so try to keep the drivers at a slow speed. Officers Norris and Burke, you're assigned to the Decker Street this morning for traffic control." Quiet laughter echoed around the room. "And, at twelve-thirty, Officers Davis and Butler, you'll relieve them. I hope you all wore your thermal underwear; it's going to be cold out there today." The room then erupted in laughter, but quickly died down.

"We also had reports of purse-snatching from customers coming out of Walmart. Officers Davis and Costa, make sure you drive through the parking lot several times during your shift today. I also need a volunteer to speak to the second-grade class at Witchcraft Hill Elementary today at nine-o'clock. I know its early in the year, but you'll be talking about bicycle safety. The principal said many of the kids got bikes for Christmas and are anxious to try them out."

"I'll do that," Officer Scott volunteered.

"Thanks, Charlene. I appreciate that." He jotted something down on his notepad. "Detective Perry, I'm glad to see you joining us today. Do you have anything to add to the briefing?"

Nathan hadn't expected to be called upon and was taken by surprise. All eyes were upon him.

"I really don't have anything to add, only that I appreciate all the help that I've received from everyone with my cases."

"Thank you, detective," the sergeant replied. "Okay, that's the highlights. Pick up your patrol sheets as you go out the door. Hit the streets."

The officers got up and headed out to begin their shift. Nathan waited by the door for Hank to walk by. "Can I talk to you for a minute?"

"Sure," Hank replied.

"Wait for me in my office. I need to speak to the sergeant and then I'll be in."

Hank left the room and Nathan stepped to the podium where Donnelly stood looking through some papers.

"Sergeant, I'd like to take Office Wheeler with me today when I go to speak with Charlene Miller, the murder victim's wife."

He looked up. "Gloria Wheeler?"

"Yes. I believe Officer Wheeler would be a big help with the interview. Sometimes, police work needs a woman's touch and I think this is one of those times."

"If she can find someone to cover the front desk while she's gone, I suppose it's okay."

"Thank you, Sergeant."

Nathan went back to his office where Hank stood looking at the certificates on the wall. "Thanks for waiting." He sat down and put his coffee on the desk, and Hank took a seat also. "What do you know about a PI named Joe Cassidy?"

"Joe? You remember Joe from high school. He was one of the student managers of the football team."

"Was he kind of a dopey kid? He never really knew what he was supposed to do unless someone told him."

"That's him," Hank said.

"Does he know what he's doing as a private investigator?"

"Mostly, people hire him for divorce cases or a lawyer will have him do some legwork on a case. He has an office between the Library and City Hall. Why do you ask?"

Nathan took a drink from his coffee mug and then sat it back on his desk. "Chief Cabot told me to let him look at the case files from the burglaries because we aren't making any progress."

"Seriously?" Hank tried to hold back a chuckle. "Who hired him?"

"The Homeowners Association at the mayor's suggestion.

Does he even make a living as a PI around here?"

"Nah, he doesn't get enough jobs for that, but his parent left him a pretty large amount of money to live off of. John Hawkins, the City Clerk, is in charge of it. Joe would blow it all, if Hawkins didn't manage it for him."

"Why Hawkins? What's the connection?" Nathan asked.

"Hawkins was Joe's parent's attorney."

"Hawkins is an attorney, why's he the City Clerk then? Does it pay that well?"

"He's still an attorney, but not very good. He gets paid for handling Joe's trust fund. That and the salary as clerk gives him enough income without having to work as hard as he would as a lawyer. Are you going to let Joe see the case files?"

Nathan let out a deep breath. "Not if I can help it, but I have a feeling he'll be reporting back to the mayor, who will then call the chief."

Gloria appeared at Nathan's door. "Daniel Grant's office called and said the warrant you needed for the bank video is ready."

"You could have called me on the phone to tell me that."

"I needed a break."

"I can pick up the warrant and serve it, if you want," Hank offered.

"That would be great. Thanks," Nathan said. Gloria started to leave. "Wait, Gloria. I have a job for you."

"What do you need?"

"I'm going to visit Charlene Miller today to ask her a few questions and I'd like for you to come with me."

"Really?" Her eyes lit up, and then she gave him a skeptical look. "The chief will never let me be away from the front desk."

"I already cleared it with Sergeant Donnelly. He said if you can find someone to cover for you, you could go."

"I'm sure I can find someone."

Nathan could practically see the wheels turning in her head. "I'd like to go right after lunch."

"I'll be ready." She rushed away.

Hank laughed and Nathan was pleased that he was helping Gloria do some actual fieldwork.

"I'd better go take care of that warrant," Hank said.

"Thanks." After Hank left, Nathan got the case files out for the burglaries and took them to the copy machine down the hall. He only made copies of things in the files that he wanted to share with Cassidy. If the chief found out he wasn't giving him the whole file, there'd be hell to pay.

He finished the copying and picked up some blank file folders and went back to his office to assemble. Five files and one cup of coffee later, he was finished. He bound the files with a couple rubber bands and placed them in his drawer.

Wanting to get it over with, he picked up the phone and dialed Cassidy's phone number.

"Cassidy Investigations. Joe speaking." Nathan cringed, hearing the name of Joe's company.

"Joe, this is Nathan Perry."

"I was hoping you'd call soon. When can I get a look at those case files?"

Nathan turned his chair to look out the window. "That's what I was calling about. I've made copies of the files for--"

"That's great!" Cassidy interrupted. "I'll be right over."

Nathan could hear the excitement in his voice and didn't want to deal with Cassidy today. "I'm getting ready to leave on another matter. I'll leave them at the front desk for you this afternoon."

"At the front desk? Well, I thought maybe we could go over the files together, in case I have any questions."

Nathan let out a breath. "Sure, Joe. Will you be at your office over lunch?"

"I will."

"I'll drop them off around noon."

"Great. I'll be waiting. I'm really looking forward to working with you on this, Nathan."

"See you then." He turned back to his desk and hung up

the phone. This was not going to turn out well. He thought Joe seemed a little too enthusiastic about this and wasn't looking forward to working with him at all.

Nathan stood to stretch his legs and took a walk to the break room. He noticed Ryan Avery sitting at a table working on a report. After rinsing out his cup, he took a seat across from him. "Morning, Ryan. How's your day going?"

The young officer looked up from the laptop computer he was typing on. "It's been busy already. The mayor's wife called in about some guy harassing her at her home on Mano Island. By the time I got there, the guy was gone."

"That doesn't sound like a busy morning to me."

"It wouldn't have been, but he really scared her and she insisted I walk around her house and the neighborhood looking for him."

"She wanted you to walk the neighborhood?"

"She said the guy left on foot when she was finally able to close her door."

"Did she say what the guy wanted?"

"She said he kept insisting on seeing the mayor. She tried to tell him to go to City Hall, but he kept saying the mayor wasn't there, so he knew he must be home."

"I assume she gave you a good description?"

"Yes, sir." I walked around that island for about an hour and didn't see anyone matching the description."

"Can you email your report when you're finished with it? I think I should follow up with Mrs. Newcomb. I'm sure the mayor will be calling the chief and it will be better if I'm already looking into it."

"Yes, sir. I'm just proofreading it now and will get it right to you," Avery said.

"Thanks." After relieving himself in the bathroom, Nathan decided to change his drink. He walked to the soda machine, dropping several coins in and pushing the button for a Coke. He walked back into his office just as his computer dinged with an email. He sat down and opened the report from Avery. While waiting for it to print, he twisted open the bottle and took a long drink.

When the printer stopped, Nathan gathered the copies and read through them, making a few notes in the margin and a few more in his notebook.

It was near eleven o'clock when Nathan closed the file, putting it inside his notebook. He dialed Gloria's extension, but got a busy signal, so he walked down to the front desk. It looked like a typical Monday with the lobby fairly full. He waited for Gloria to finish her phone call.

"Mrs. Carson, I spoke with Sergeant Donnelly after your first visit and he assured me he would have an officer drive by your home--" Gloria looked up at Nathan and shrugged her shoulders. "Yes, ma'am. I'll mention it again and will personally see to it that an officer watches your home tonight." She wrote something down on a note pad. "Thank you, Mrs. Carson. Have a nice day." She hung up the phone.

"Is that the same lady that was in here a few days ago complaining about some kids?" Nathan asked.

"It is. She's a nice lady and lives alone with nothing to do but look out her window and snoop on her neighbors. That's probably why the kids are bothering her. My husband heard at school that whenever the boys bring their dates home in the neighborhood, they always see her curtain move to the side and her face peeking through the window to watch them."

Nathan laughed. "No boy or girl wants to be watched during the goodnight kiss."

"Exactly."

"I'm going to drop those burglary files off at Joe Cassidy's. I decided it would be better to take them to him than have him stop by here and not be able to get rid of him. I'll be back after I grabbed something to eat at my house. If you'll be ready, we can go visit Charlene Miller when I get back."

"I'll be ready."

Nathan went back to his office for the files, his coat, and gloves. After taking the detour around the water main break, he found a parking spot nearby Cassidy's office. He opened the door to the dinging of a bell and stepped inside.

He found the front office empty. No secretary at the desk and no clients seated at the couch.

"Can I help you? Oh, Nathan, it's good to see you," Cassidy said stepping out from a rear office.

"I brought the files for you." He held the folders out to him.

"Thanks. Please come back to my office and I'll give them a quick glance." Cassidy took the files and started back to his office. Nathan followed. "Please sit down."

"I don't have much time."

"Oh, this will only take me a minute. I just want to make sure I understand how you set up your files. I'll give them a better look later and then we can get together to discuss the case. Maybe over dinner one night this week." Cassidy sat down behind his desk.

Nathan reluctantly sat down. There was no way he was going to eat a meal with this guy. He watched him thumb through the files and wondered if he'd ever even looked at a police report before.

"I don't see any photos. Weren't any pictures taken at the crime scenes? I also don't see the file for the burglary at the newspaper office." He looked up at Nathan.

Damn. "Photos take a little longer to copy. I'll let you know when I have them for you. As for the burglary at the newspaper office, it's been classified as an assault since the security guard was hurt. We really don't think it's connected to the Mano Island burglaries."

"Well, okay."

Nathan could tell he was disappointed that he didn't get that file.

"There's nothing here about Raymond Miller's murder." Cassidy noted.

"The information pertaining to the murder is going to have to remain classified. I'm sorry."

"I'll have to mention that to the chief."

"You go right ahead, Joe. But, I can give both Chief Cabot and the mayor several reasons why that information should remain confidential. To start with, I don't think the State Police would like that information released to a private citizen."

"The State Police are involved?" he asked.

"Yes, they're assisting and doing a lot of the legwork in Boston." Nathan hoped that satisfied his curiosity.

Cassidy looked back down at the files and then up at Nathan again. "I'll study these in more detail when I have a little more time. When you get the photos for me, we'll sit down and discuss the cases. Sound good?"

"That would be fine, Joe." Nathan stood to leave.

"I was surprised to see you and Dana together the other night."

"Why is that?"

"Well, high school was a long time ago and I'm sure things have happened in your life. I know they have in Dana's. She was pretty heartbroken when you just up and left after high school without so much as a word to her."

"Like you said, high school was a long time ago." With that, he walked out of the office and back to his car.

As he drove to his house for some lunch, he thought about Cassidy's comment about things happening in Dana's life and wondered what he meant. The sky had cleared, and the sun shone brightly now, but the temperature still hovered around the freezing mark.

Nathan parked the car in his driveway and went inside. Lunch would have to be a sandwich today with no leftovers in the refrigerator. He grabbed a plastic bag of ham and some Swiss cheese and put together a sandwich on rye bread with mayo.

He sat at his kitchen table, looked at his watch, and decided to call Katherine, hoping to catch her on her lunch hour. After two rings, she answered.

"Hello."

"Hi Kath, it's Nathan."

"Nathan? Is something wrong?"

"No, nothing's wrong. I thought I'd call and catch you on your lunch hour to see how you were." He took a bite of his sandwich.

"I'm fine. I actually took an early lunch today and am heading back to work now. We're really booked with appointments. I suppose you're busy today too?"

He swallowed. "I am. The department is still working on that murder case and I'm going to go interview the widow this afternoon."

"That's got to be difficult for her. Be nice when you talk with her."

"I'm always nice. Besides, I'm taking a female officer with me and will likely let her ask most of the questions. You'd like her. She's a strong woman that wants to do more than just work the front desk at the department, but the chief is the type of person that doesn't think women belong out on the street."

"How do you get along with him?"

"Why would you ask that?"

"Well, you do have a little history with authority figures." She gave a little chuckle.

"That doctor didn't know what he was doing. Anyway, the chief and I get along just fine. He's old school, but he's the boss. What more can I say?"

"Nathan, I just parked back at work. I have to go now. It was good hearing from you."

There was something in her voice that didn't sound right. "Kath, is everything okay? You don't sound like yourself."

"Well, like I said we're really busy and I'm working more hours. I've not been sleeping very well lately, but I'm fine. Really, I am."

"Get some rest, okay?"

"I promise. Nathan?"

"Yes."

"Thanks for calling."

"You call me anytime you need something," he said.

"I will. Goodbye."

"Bye." He ended the call and took another bite of his sandwich.

He knew something was wrong with Katherine. He wished he could go see her, but knew that was impossible with his workload and probably not a good idea anyway. They each had their own lives now. Nathan finished his sandwich and grabbed a soda from the refrigerator before heading back to the police department.

Gloria met him at his office door when he entered the building. "I'm ready."

"How did you know I was back?"

"Melinda in Radio told me when she saw you on the surveillance camera drive into the rear parking lot. She's covering the front desk for me while I'm gone."

"Just let me get my notebook." He walked into his office and, with his back to Gloria, smiled at her enthusiasm. He checked his voicemail for messages and found none. "Let's go," he said after picking up his notebook and a case file.

"Thank you," Gloria blurted out on the drive to Mano Island.

"For what?"

"For giving me a chance to do real police work. I only hope you don't get into trouble with the chief for it."

"I told you I cleared it with Donnelly."

"That doesn't mean the chief will approve."

"Let me worry about that. When we speak with Mrs. Miller, I want you to introduce me and then you to take the lead of the questioning."

"Me? I wouldn't know what to ask."

"You read the file, right?"

"Yes."

"Just remember your police training. If there's anything

you miss, I'll follow up. You'll do fine." He pulled the car into the Miller driveway and they got out.

"You're sure you want me to do this?" Gloria asked.

"Positive."

They walked to the front door and Nathan pushed the doorbell and then took a step back, letting Gloria stand in front of the door.

When the door opened, a pale woman with slightly bloodshot eyes looked at them. It was obvious she had been crying. "Can I help you?"

"Are you Mrs. Miller?" Gloria asked.

"Yes."

"I'm Officer Gloria Wheeler and this is Detective Nathan Perry. I believe Detective Perry called about us coming to speak with you today."

"Yes, please come in."

Mrs. Miller led them to the living room. "Won't you have a seat? Can I get you something to drink?"

"No, thank you," Gloria said.

"Nothing for me," Nathan added.

Mrs. Miller and Gloria sat on the couch, and Nathan took the chair near to Gloria.

"We're so sorry for your loss," Gloria started with first.

"Thank you."

"You understand we have to ask you some questions for our investigation."

"I understand," she responded.

"Where was your husband coming from that night?" Gloria asked.

"It was his scheduled night to work late. He volunteers to do the accounting at the Mystic Theater Company. Wednesday night is when he finalizes the accounts from the weekend performances for the bank deposit the following day."

"You weren't home either. Where were you?"

"I volunteer at the senior center on the nights that

Raymond works late. We usually get home around the same time."

"What time is that?"

"Around nine o'clock."

"But, he got home early that night. Do you know why?" Gloria asked.

"The theater was closed over the weekend because they are working on a new play, so there were no deposits. He told me he only needed to update the accounts." She wiped a tear from her eye. "He called me at seven forty-five to say he was on his way home." Her voiced cracked. "I left the center at eight and found him twenty minutes later."

Gloria reached over and patted Mrs. Miller's hand. "It's okay. I know this is hard. Please take your time." She looked at Nathan, who took over the questioning.

"Mrs. Miller, did your husband ever bring home any of the money for the deposits for the theater?"

"No. He either dropped it off in the night deposit, or someone from the theater took it the next day." She looked up at Nathan. "Do you think they were after that money?"

"We don't know. Was his schedule pretty routine?"

Yes," she paused. "Until that night." She broke down crying.

They waited until she composed herself before continuing. "One last question," Nathan said. "Do you know if anyone made any threats to your husband, or even yourself?"

"No one has threatened me and if anyone had threatened Raymond, he didn't tell me about it."

"Thank you, Mrs. Miller. We're so sorry to have to bother you like this. If we have any more questions, we'll call," Nathan said, standing.

Gloria stood also, and they walked to the door, followed by Mrs. Miller.

"Please find the person who did this," she begged.

"We'll do our best," Gloria answered.

She and Nathan left the house.

"Did you figure anything out from that?" Gloria asked.

"Did you?"

"We need to check the camera at the bank to see if he made the deposit. If there was no deposit made, then someone from the theater might be involved."

"Very good. We'll to talk to someone at the theater, and the bank, but not today. I have one more stop to make before we leave the island."

"Where's that?"

"I want to talk to the mayor's wife. She had an aggressive visitor this morning and I want to find out more about that. The file is there on the seat, if you want to read the report."

"Oh my, is she okay?" Gloria picked up the file and started reading.

Nathan started the car and drove down the street toward the Newcomb home. "I think she was scared, but nothing more." He turned into the circular driveway and parked in front of the mansion of a house. He and Gloria got out and walked to the front door. "Take the lead on the questioning here too." Nathan pushed the doorbell.

He pushed it a second time before a voice was heard from behind the door. "Who is it?"

"It's Detective Perry and Officer Wheeler from the Mystic Police Department. We'd like to speak with you about the intruder you had this morning," Nathan said.

"One moment. Can you move over to the window and let me see your badge?"

Nathan and Gloria stepped to the window closest to the door. Gloria was in uniform and Nathan held his badge up for her to see when she pushed the curtains to the side. After seeing them, she moved away from the window and the front door opened.

"I'm sorry, but I don't open the door for anyone until I know who they are. Please come in."

Nathan and Gloria stepped inside, and Mrs. Newcomb closed and locked the door behind them. "Right this way."

She led them into the living room and they all sat down.

"Would you like some coffee?" she asked, nodding her head toward her cup on the table in front of them. "It's so cold out today."

Both of the officers declined, and Gloria started the questioning. "I've read the report about the intruder and we just wanted to follow up on it. Can you tell me as exact as possible what the man said?"

She took a sip of her coffee. Her hand trembled. "There was a pounding on the door. I thought it might be a neighbor with something wrong with all the burglaries happening. I opened it to find this man demanding to see Robert."

"Can you remember exactly what he said to you?" Gloria asked.

"He said, 'I need to see Newcomb. I know he's here.' Then, he started shouting his name like Robert was here. I told him he was at City Hall, but he wouldn't believe me."

"Did he try to come into the house?" Gloria asked as Nathan took notes during the interview.

"Not at first, but when he took a step toward the door, I started to close it. That's when he tried."

"How did you keep him out?"

"I'm not sure. I think he was distracted by something. Yes, a car drove by and he looked toward the street. When he did, I was able to close the door and lock it."

"Did he leave then?" Nathan asked.

"No, he started beating on the door and shouted that he knew Robert was not at work. He demanded to see him. That's when I called the police. I told the man through the door that I had called them and he left."

"Do you know if he had a weapon?" Gloria asked.

"I didn't see one."

"What did he look like?" Nathan asked.

"I told that other officer. Why do you need to know the same thing?"

"We need to double-check everything and that includes

information you've already reported. Sometimes a victim remembers something new when questioned a second time, like you remembering the car that drove by."

"I understand. I'm sorry. I think he was about six-foot tall, same as my husband. He had dark hair, brown eyes, and was maybe in his late twenties. He was wearing jeans and a green t-shirt."

"Did the man park his car in the driveway? Nathan asked.

"No, I didn't see one. He left on foot."

"About the car that drove by, did you see it, or know who drove by?" Nathan asked.

"I'm not sure. Maybe one of the kids down the street. With the way our driveway is, it's hard to see from the front door, but I remember the car was really loud."

"I think we've bothered you enough for the day. Thank you for your assistance, Mrs. Newcomb," Nathan said, standing. Gloria stood also.

"Do you think you can find him?" she asked.

"We'll do everything we can and your additional information about the car driving by will help."

Mrs. Newcomb showed them to the front door.

"You really should have a peephole installed in your door," Nathan suggested.

"My husband has already ordered a new door with one in it, but thank you for your concern and thank you for coming by today. It's certainly nice to know that the police department is on the job."

"Thank you again, Mrs. Newcomb." Nathan and Gloria stepped outside and walked to their car.

Nathan turned the windshield wipers on intermittent as it was beginning to drizzle rain on the drive back to the police department.

"What now?" Gloria asked.

"I'll talk to Officer Avery about a loud car some kid drives on the island and see if he's familiar. I'd also like to check with the mayor's office to see if that man stopped by their office to see the mayor before going to his home."

"Do you think he's dangerous?" Gloria asked.

"You never know, but I'd like to pin him down before he tries to see the mayor again, whether it be at City Hall or at his home."

"What about the thefts and the murder out on the island? Do you think this person could have anything to do with that?"

"Probably not, but it's not something I'd rule out completely."

Once inside the police department, Gloria went back to the front desk to write up her report on the questioning of both Mrs. Wright and Mrs. Newcomb. Nathan returned to his office, where he found a pink message saying Chief Cabot wanted to see him as soon as he got back. It was marked urgent. He let out a deep breath, wondering what he did now, and headed up to see the chief.

The door to the office was open, but Nathan knocked anyway. The chief looked up. "Perry, good, come in and close the door behind you."

That can't be good, Nathan thought as he closed the door and then took a seat in front of the desk.

Cabot sat back in his chair. "I understand you went out to Mano Island to interview Charlene Miller."

"Yes, sir. I did."

"Did you learn anything new?"

"I'm not sure. I have to follow up on a few things."

"I also understand you took Gloria Wheeler with you."

"Yes, sir. I cleared that with Sergeant Donnelly this morning." Nathan squirmed in his chair.

"I don't think Gloria is ready for field work."

"I think she is ready. She did a great job interviewing Mrs. Miller and also Mrs. Newcomb."

"Mrs. Newcomb!" His eyes widened.

"Yes, sir. She had an aggressive visitor at her home this morning looking for the mayor. Officer Wheeler and I stopped by there after we finished at the Miller home to follow up on Officer Avery's report. I think both Mrs. Newcomb and Mrs. Miller would agree that Officer Wheeler showed compassion and integrity in her interviewing." Nathan now sat up straighter in his chair.

The chief briefly stuttered while trying to come up with something to say. "Well, don't do it again without clearing it with me first. Understood?"

"No, sir."

"What do you mean, 'no, sir'?" The chief leaned toward his desk.

"I mean, if I need to take Officer Wheeler with me to do another interview, I will. She was a great asset and I think both of those women felt more at ease talking with another woman."

The chief let out a deep breath while Nathan held his, waiting for Cabot's final decision.

"All right, then. Get back to work."

Nathan stood and left the office feeling pretty good about his interaction with Chief Cabot. Of course, there would be hell to pay later, as soon as the chief came up with some sort of task for him to do.

Chapter Eight

A few days after the talk with Chief Cabot, Nathan walked into the police department through the back door. After hanging his coat in his office and getting his coffee cup, he went into the morning briefing room.

Several of the officers were gathered in front of the bulletin board looking at some papers and filling in their names. "What's going on, guys?" Nathan asked.

"It's sign-ups for the department's softball team," one of the officers said.

"Softball team? It's still winter." Nathan headed to the coffeemaker.

"The town likes to get an early start on the teams to see how many will be in the league this year," another officer answered.

After filling his cup, he walked over to them. "Where do I sign?"

The group of officers looked back and forth at each other. Finally, one spoke. "Detective, you'll probably be too busy with work to deal with all the practices and games."

"Nonsense. I can work around my schedule as well as any of you."

Again, more looks between the other officers.

"What's going on? Don't you want me on the team?" he asked.

"It's not that. It's just, are you able to play? You know, with your leg and all?" one of the officers said.

Nathan was taken back with that question. "What do you mean, my leg?"

"From Afghanistan," another officer said.

"How do you know about Afghanistan?"

"It's in the article about you in today's newspaper." The officer held up the newspaper folded to the article.

Nathan snatched the paper from the officer's hand and saw Dana's name in the by-line of the article. He took the pen from one of the officers and signed his name to the list.

"There's nothing wrong with my leg." Nathan turned and marched out of the room and straight to his office where he slammed the door shut, rattling the frames on the wall.

He sat at his desk to read the article. It was all there. The IED explosion, his injuries to his leg and hearing, his surgeries, and his recovery time before coming to Mystic. Everything he had told Dana over dinner.

He was furious and embarrassed. He needed to get out of the office. He got up, grabbed his coat, and left the building.

As he drove down the street, he saw Dana walking up the street toward the café. He hit the brakes and stopped the car next to her and got out.

"Nathan, I can explain," she said, before he could say anything.

"Why would you write that stuff about me when I asked you not to?"

"I didn't write it."

"What do you mean, you didn't write it. Your name is right there on the article. I can't believe I trusted you. I should have known better than trust a reporter, especially one I slept with."

"Now, wait just a minute," Dana exclaimed. "Just because an article has a reporter's name on it doesn't mean that reporter wrote the whole article."

"You're just making excuses! Admit it, you couldn't resist

writing a big article telling all my secrets."

"Nathan, listen to me. The article I wrote didn't have anything about your injuries in it. Somehow, Benson knew about your injuries and when I refused to add it in, he must have had someone else do it, or he did it himself. I wouldn't do that to you." She touched his arm.

Nathan jerked his arm away. He looked toward The Witches Brew. "Great. We'll be the talk of the town now."

"What are you talking about?"

He looked back at her. "Everyone in the café is watching us. Our little argument must have been a good show for them."

She glanced toward the café and back at Nathan. "So, what? It's none of their business. This is between us. You do believe me, don't you? That wasn't the story I wrote."

"I don't know what to believe now." He walked back to his car and drove off. It took a drive of seven blocks down and two to the east for him to calm down a little.

Nathan parked his car in front of the Mystic Theater Company. Finding the front door locked, he walked to the alley at the side of the building and saw a side door. It was unlocked and he went inside.

Waiting a few seconds to let his eyes adjust to the darkened hallway, he heard voices coming from the front of the building and started in that direction.

The closer he got, the brighter the hallway became until he found himself next to a door that said office and knocked. It opened and inside he found four people.

"Can we help you?" the man behind the desk asked.

"Detective Nathan Perry, Mystic PD. I'm looking for whoever is in charge of the theater." He moved his jacket aside, revealing the badge on his belt, and then let his jacket fall back in place.

"That would be me," the man said. "I'm Floyd Parker, the manager. Please, come in."

Nathan looked at the other three in the office, which

was very small with little room left for him to enter.

"The three of you get out. I'll meet you on stage when I'm finished here," Parker said.

Nathan stepped back, letting the others pass, and then he entered the office.

Parker walked around his desk and cleared a pile of papers from the chair. "Have a seat. What can I do for you, Detective Perry?" He moved back around his desk and sat in his chair.

Nathan sat down. "I'm investigating Raymond Miller's death and wanted to ask you a few questions."

"Certainly. It was so tragic. What can I do to help?"

"Mrs. Miller said he was supposed to be working late here that night. Do you know what time he left?"

"I'm really not sure. I wasn't working that night. Raymond was usually the last person to leave the theater. Once the play is over, he stays late to count the money and then takes it to the night deposit at the bank on this way home."

Nathan took his notebook out and wrote something down. "Was the deposit made that night?"

"No, there was no deposit. We weren't open due to a new play being rehearsed. The cast had a short read-through and was probably gone by six-thirty."

"He worked here for two hours without any money to count? What was he doing?"

"Raymond usually uses those nights to get all of the accounts up to date and balanced. I assume that's what he was doing." Parker said.

"You saw Mr. Miller that evening?"

"I was gone for most of the day, but I saw him for a few minutes before I went home."

"What time was that?" Nathan asked.

"Probably around five-o'clock."

"Did Mr. Miller ever say anything about being nervous or having a bad feeling taking money to the night deposit alone?"

"If he did, he never said anything to me," Parker replied.

Nathan stood and gave Parker one of his cards. "I think I have everything I need. If you think of anything else, please call me."

"I will. Say, we're having a dinner theater presentation this Saturday, would you be interested in some tickets? They're free for you, detective." He opened the drawer of his desk and brought out two tickets.

"I couldn't accept free tickets, but I wouldn't mind paying for them." He reached for his wallet in his back pocket. "What's the play?"

"It's a comedic mystery called Murder in the Air."

Nathan sort of chuckled to himself. "Sounds like a good one. Can you take a credit card?"

"We sure can, follow me."

Parker walked out of his office and to the box office where the credit card machine was. He took Nathan's card, pushed a few buttons on the machine, and the receipt printed out. "Do you want a matinee or evening performance? I will tell you, the evening performance will have the best menu."

"Evening will work better for me." He signed the receipt and handed it back to Parker.

"Thank you and I'll see you Saturday night."

"I'm looking forward to it." Nathan put his card in his wallet and the tickets in his pocket.

"Detective?"

"Yes."

"I read the article in the newspaper about you this morning and well, I just want to say that I can't tell you have any problems at all with your hearing."

Nathan wasn't surprised that this was already coming up. "I don't have a problem with my hearing, or with my leg. Both problems have healed and I'm fine now."

"That's good."

Nathan turned and left the theater the same way he came in. As he walked out of the alley to his car, he thought the dinner theater might be a good peace offering to Dana. His temper didn't show often, but he let it get the better of him when he saw her this morning, and he needed to make amends.

Before going back to the office, he decided to stop by the mayor's office. Traffic was light for a Tuesday morning, especially with the sunny weather. He drove down the street toward City Hall. He never could figure out why City Hall was so far away from the police department.

At the next light, he turned right and then left into the parking lot. The mayor's office was located on the top floor of the old three-story building. After getting off of the elevator, he opened the door to the office and walked in.

"Good morning. Can I help you?" the secretary said.

"I'm Detective Perry from the Mystic Police Department. Would it be possible for me to see the mayor for a few minutes? It's about the incident at his home yesterday morning."

"I'm sorry, the mayor is out this morning. He should be back this afternoon, if you'd like to make an appointment."

He looked at his watch. "Maybe you can help me. Did a man stop here yesterday morning insisting on seeing the mayor?"

"We get a lot of people in here wanting to see the mayor, Detective. You included."

Nathan smiled. "Point taken. This gentleman would have probably been more aggressive."

"There was a man here yesterday that was a little demanding, but I told him Mayor Newcomb wasn't in. Like I said to you, I suggested he make an appointment, but he just turned and left without saying a word."

"The mayor wasn't here at that time either?" Nathan asked.

"No, he wasn't scheduled to be in his office until after lunch."

"Where was he?" Nathan took his notebook out to jot down something.

"I can't tell you that. The mayor's schedule is not open to the public."

"Well, I'm not exactly the public, now am I?"

The secretary smiled. "I suppose you aren't, but I'm still not allowed to give out his schedule." She motioned Nathan to come closer and whispered, "To be honest, I don't know where the mayor was yesterday morning. That is happening more and more lately too, but please don't tell anyone I said that."

"I won't say a word. Can you tell me this? Did he come in on time in the afternoon?"

She hesitated. "Yes, he did."

"Thank you. You've been very helpful." He turned to leave.

"You don't need to see Mayor Newcomb after all?"

Nathan turned back to her. "Just tell him I was here. I'm sure he'll be in contact with me when he hears that."

As he left the mayor's office, Nathan decided to take the stairs down instead of the elevator. He looked up and down the hallway before descending, taking notice of the security cameras near the ceiling. On the first floor, he stopped by the City Clerk's office.

"Good morning, Detective Perry," the man behind the counter said.

It took Nathan a few seconds, but he finally remembered him as John Hawkins, the City Clerk he met when he and Hank visited the Chamber of Commerce office. "Mr. Hawkins, right?"

"Yes." The two men shook hands. "What brings you to my office today?"

"Yesterday morning, there was a gentleman that visited the mayor's office that may have later caused an incidence. I noticed the hallways have cameras. Could you tell me where I would go to look at the security video from yesterday?"

Hawkins walked around the end of the counter. "Besides the guard at the door, there's also a guard on duty in the security office to watch the monitors. I'll show you the way." He led Nathan out of his office and down the hall to the rear of the building.

Next to the employee entrance was a glassed-in room with a door marked Security. Nathan could see a man sitting at a desk with several monitors above him. Hawkins knocked on the door and the guard opened it.

"Bill, this is Detective Perry from the police department. He needs to see the surveillance video from yesterday," Hawkins said.

"Certainly, please come in and I'll pull it up for you, Detective Perry." The guard walked back to his desk and sat down. Nathan and Hawkins stood behind him when he started typing on the computer.

"How long is the video looped before it is written over?" Nathan asked.

"Sounds like you're familiar with security footage"

"Somewhat."

"We keep the video on the hard drive for two weeks before it's written over again. What time of day do you want and which camera?"

"First thing yesterday morning at the mayor's office," Nathan said.

The guard typed a few more things. "Here we go."

Nathan leaned over the guard to see the monitor, as did Hawkins. It showed a man entering the mayor's office, and then, about five minutes later, the video went blank.

"What happened to the picture?" Hawkins asked. He and Nathan straightened up.

The guard started typing again. "We've been having problems with that camera going in and out for weeks. The first couple times that happened, I went running up thinking something was wrong. Once I checked the camera, I found that it was just a malfunction. We really need a new camera up there."

"Why don't you get it replaced?" Nathan asked.

"We don't have it in the budget for this year," the guard replied.

"It seems that you'd want your best camera on the mayor's office," Nathan commented.

"Yes, sir. You're right about that." The guard looked at Hawkins.

"Our budget is already stretched thin, but I'll mention it to the mayor again and see if we can find the money for it somewhere," Hawkins said.

"Bill, can you record the segment of that man walking into the mayor's office and send it to me at the police department?"

"Sure. I'll put it on a flashdrive and can even drop it off over my lunch hour today."

"That would be great. Thanks." Nathan left the office with Hawkins right behind him. Out in the hallway, he stopped. "John, thank you for your help today. I do appreciate it."

"Anytime you need anything, just let me know." Hawkins slapped Nathan on the back, like they were old friends.

Nathan left and drove back to the police department. Hank was waiting for him when he came in.

"I got the surveillance video from the bank ATM, " Hank said.

"Have you looked at it yet?

"Not yet. I just got it." He followed Nathan into his office.

"Well, let's take a look." Nathan sat at his desk and logged onto his computer. Hank gave him a DVD and Nathan loaded it on the computer. A few seconds later, the video began to play.

The men watched intently as they saw a tall man wearing a dark hoodie climb a ladder, remove the sign at the Church Street Deli, and then rush down the street.

"He never looked at the camera." Hank said.

"No, but we at least have an idea how tall the person is."

"There was only one person. At the newspaper office there were two men." Hank moved around to the front of the desk.

Nathan rubbed his chin. "That is a problem. Obviously, we're dealing with more than one person." He removed the disk from his computer and handed it back to Hank. "Will you take this to Mallory and have her log it in as evidence. Ask her to view the whole video to see if anything else shows up we might be able to use."

"Will do, boss." Hank left.

Nathan took out his notebook and looked through his notes from both interviews with Mrs. Miller and Mrs. Newcomb. When he heard a knock at his door, he looked up to see Officer Avery standing there.

"Ryan, come in."

He took a step into the office. "Gloria said you wanted to see me."

"Yes. Sit down."

"What can I do for you, sir?"

"Gloria and I went out to see Mrs. Newcomb today and she said there was a car that drove by while the subject was there to see her husband." He thumbed through the pages until he got to where he wrote down the information from the interview.

"She didn't say anything to me about that."

"She just remembered it today. She didn't see the car, but heard it because it was so loud. Does that sound like any cars you know of on the island?" Nathan asked.

The young officer thought for a few seconds. "There are a few teenagers that live out there that have souped-up their cars. I can park at the bridge and watch as the kids come home from school this afternoon to see if I can find the car."

"That would be a big help. If you can figure out who it was, we need to know if they saw anything."

"Will do." The officer stood and left the office.

Nathan picked up the phone receiver and dialed Gloria's extension number. After several rings she answered.

"Officer Wheeler."

"Gloria, it's Nathan. Around lunch today, the security guard from the Town Hall is supposed to bring a flashdrive of a video of someone that tried to see the Mayor yesterday. When he delivers it, could you have him sign it in as evidence and then could you call Mrs. Newcomb and ask her to come down here to view the video to see if it might be her intruder?"

"When do you want her here?"

"This afternoon, if possible. When you know what time she'll be here, let me know."

"I'll call her right now."

Nathan hung up the phone and then picked the receiver right back up and dialed another number.

"*The Mystic Messenger*, can I help you?"

"Can I speak to Dana Tyler, please?"

"Who's calling?"

"This is Nathan Perry."

"One moment, Detective Perry and I'll connect you."

Nathan was amused that the receptionist knew who he was. She must have read the article in the newspaper.

You've reached the voicemail of Dana Tyler. Please leave your name and number and a brief message and I'll try to return your call as soon as I can. Thank you.

Nathan hung up the phone. Then, he tried her cell phone. After a few rings, it went to voicemail also. He didn't think apologizing to Dana via her voicemail was the right way to do it, and she probably wouldn't return his call if he asked. He needed to see her in person to ask her about going to the theater.

Nathan's computer dinged, indicating an email arrived. He saw it was from Mallory and opened it. She had logged and reviewed the ATM video that Hank took to her and determined that the subject was approximately six-foot, two inches tall. Nathan emailed back, thanking her, and asked if she could print a photo of the subject from the video.

Gloria appeared at the door. "Nathan, I spoke with Mrs. Newcomb and she will be here right after lunch to look at the video."

"Did you have any problems getting her to come?"

"No, she seemed very eager to look at the video. Not at all like she was when we visited with her."

"Maybe she's calmed down by now. Ryan Avery is watching for that loud car out on the island today and will let us know what he finds."

"That's good." Gloria still stood in the doorway.

"Is there something else?" Nathan asked.

"Yes, there actually is." She stepped in and took a seat in front of his desk. He now saw that she was holding some printed papers.

"What do you have?"

"I didn't want to tell you until I had something, but I've been doing some internet research at home about sign burglaries and I found something."

"Go on." Nathan sat back in his chair.

"Well, a couple years ago over in Salem, there was a rash of burglaries where the only thing stolen were signs."

"That sounds familiar."

"Doesn't it though. The police department over there recovered a few of the signs that they found in some antique stores in Boston."

"Was an arrest made?" Nathan asked.

"No, there wasn't." She looked disappointed. "But I was thinking that if we took a look at their files maybe we could see something that they missed, or something similar to our cases. What do you think?"

"I think you're onto something. Call them and see if they'll send us a copy of their files." Nathan sat back up toward his desk and Gloria still sat in her chair. "There's more?"

"Do you think I could go over and pick the files up when they have them ready?"

Nathan closed his eyes, looked down, and then looked back up at Gloria. "I don't think that would be a very good idea. The chief sort of raked me over the coals about taking you with me to do those interviews this morning."

Gloria stood up. "I knew it. I knew it. I told you he wouldn't like it. I'm so sorry I got you into trouble." She was pacing.

"Gloria." She wasn't listening.

"I knew I shouldn't have gone with you."

He got up and held her by the shoulders. "Gloria. I'm not in trouble. I had Sergeant Donnelly's permission. You did very well with those interviews and that's exactly what I told the chief."

"Really?"

"Yes, and I also told him I would take you again, if the situation called for it."

"Thank you. I needed to hear that."

He dropped his hands and Gloria stood straight and tall. "Call the Salem PD and ask about those files. If it sounds like something that could help us, ask them to send them to you. I'm sure they'll expedite the process."

"I'll call them right now. Thanks, again."

"I'll always have your back."

Gloria left the office and Nathan sat back down at this desk. He felt drained after that little pep talk, but he was pleased that he was able to make her feel better about her work at the department.

Nathan worked on cases at his desk through lunch, only having a candy bar and a bottle of water for his noon meal. Around one-thirty, his phone rang. "Detective Perry."

"It's Gloria. Mrs. Newcomb is here to view the video."

"Thanks. Did Mallory get the video set up in the AV room?"

"Yes, she did."

"Great. Will you take Mrs. Newcomb there and wait with her until I get there? It should only be a few minutes."

"Yes, sir." Gloria replied.

Nathan hung up the phone. He wanted the chief in on this and took the elevator up to the second floor.

He knocked on the door frame to the office and the chief looked up. "Perry, what do you need?"

"Sir, Mrs. Newcomb is here to look at a video we have that might have her intruder on it. I thought you might want to join us."

"Why, yes. I think I would like to do that." He got up, and he and Nathan took the elevator down to the first floor and then continued into the AV room.

The chief entered first, nearly pushing Nathan aside. "Mrs. Newcomb, how are you?"

"I'm much better now than I was yesterday, Chief Cabot," she said.

"Can I get you something?" The chief looked up at Gloria. "Would you get Mrs. Newcomb some coffee?"

"No, I'm fine. Nothing for me," Mrs. Newcomb said.

Nathan looked at Gloria, who looked like she was about to explode and understandably so. "Mrs. Newcomb, we have a video of a man that was at your husband's office Tuesday morning that we believe may be the person who came to your house. I'd like for you to look at the video and tell us if it's the same person."

"Certainly."

Nathan started the video on the monitor and everyone in the room watched.

"That's him!" She pointed at the screen. "That's the man that was at my house. So, you know who he is?" She looked at Nathan.

"Not yet, but at least we now know who to look for," Nathan said.

The chief then stepped up. "Mrs. Newcomb, rest assured that we will find out who this man is and arrest him so he won't bother you again."

She stood. "Thank you, Chief Cabot. I know you will." She started to leave, but stopped next to Gloria and turned to the chief. "I told my husband what a wonderful person Officer Wheeler was yesterday during her visit. I'm afraid I was still a little rattled after the incident, but she calmed me right down. You have a good officer here, Paul," she said, looking at Gloria.

Nathan could see Gloria was just beaming.

"Well – ah – thank you. We take pride in all of our officers," the chief muttered.

"Thank you so much for your help, ma'am. We'll let you know if we need anything else and, of course, if we identify him," Nathan said.

"I'll show you the way out, Mrs. Newcomb," Gloria said. She and the mayor's wife left the room.

Nathan looked at the chief and just smiled. The chief was not amused and marched past Nathan on his way out of the room. Nathan couldn't help but laugh, once he knew Chief Cabot was out of hearing range. He then went to the front desk to see Gloria.

"Oh, Nathan did you see the look on the chief's face when Mrs. Newcomb said those nice things about me?" Gloria said.

"I did. I told you that you did a wonderful job yesterday and now the chief knows it too."

"I just hope it doesn't come back to bite me in the butt."

"We'll tackle that, if it happens. I'm going to drive out to Mano Island and then head home a little early today. If anything comes up, you can reach me on my cell phone."

"Have a good evening. See you tomorrow." Gloria sat back at the front desk and Nathan went back to his office. He put some files in his briefcase, locked his desk, and picked up his coat. The sun was shining, but he knew it was still cold out. He closed his door and headed out the back to his truck.

Driving out to Mano Island, he crossed the bridge and saw Officer Avery sitting on the side of the road and pulled up next to him. "Afternoon Ryan, any luck finding the car yet?"

"Not yet. School gets out soon and if it's a teenager, they'll have to pass me to get home."

"Good luck. Let me know tomorrow, if you find out anything." Avery gave him a little wave, and Nathan backed his truck around and drove back over the bridge.

Before going home, he thought he would stop by *The Witch's Brew* and see if Dana might be there. They didn't look too busy when Nathan parked his truck. He entered through the door and looked around. No Dana. He walked back to the counter and took a seat on one of the stools.

Ginger came out from the kitchen. "What can I get you today?"

"Nothing today. I'm looking for Dana. Have you seen her?"

"She hasn't been in since you two had your little spat Tuesday. I'm sure she was embarrassed and probably doesn't want to show her face here. Everyone in here was watching. What was your argument about anyway?" She poured Nathan a cup of coffee.

"I didn't order that."

"It's on the house. Now, tell me about your fight."

Nathan took a drink of the coffee. "It wasn't really a fight. Did you see the article about me in the newspaper that morning?"

"Yeah. I had no idea you'd been injured over there."

"Only Dana and Chief Cabot knew, or so I thought. Dana promised me she wouldn't write about it, but when I saw that article with her byline, I thought she betrayed me. Then, when I saw her on the sidewalk, I just lost it with her. I shouldn't have done it and I need to apologize to her." He took another drink of coffee. "There has to be another reason why the information about me was in that article."

Ginger laughed. "You better do more than apologize to her. You owe her big time."

"I know, but she won't answer when I call and I don't want to do it with a voicemail."

Ginger turned and looked at the clock behind the counter and then back at Nathan. "You could probably catch her in about fifteen minutes at the Witch Museum on Canal Street."

"Why would she be there?"

"For the witchcraft class," Ginger said.

Nathan gave Ginger a skeptical look. "Witchcraft class?"

"She told me she's doing a story for the paper about it. They meet once a week."

Nathan took one last drink of coffee. "Thanks, Ginger. You're the best."

Rushing out the door, Nathan headed toward Canal Street. Finding a parking spot proved difficult. *The witchcraft class must be popular,* he thought.

Finally, he spotted an empty parking place and pulled his truck in, shutting off the engine. He got out and started walking toward the museum when he spotted a flower vendor across the street. He crossed and bought a colorful bouquet of Gerbera daisies. He paid the vendor and crossed the street just as a group of women were coming out of the museum.

He watched as each woman came out, but didn't see Dana. As the last one walked out, he stopped her. "Is Dana Tyler still in there?"

"Dana? She left about twenty minutes ago," the lady replied.

"She didn't happen to say where she was going, did she?"

"No. I'm sorry."

"Thanks." Nathan walked back to his truck and placed the flowers on the seat and drove to the Capt's Waterfront Bar and Grill. When he pulled into the parking lot, he spotted Dana's car. Maybe the day would end on a good note after all. He picked up the flowers and went into the bar.

He spotted Dana sitting at the same booth they had shared on the first night of his new job. She had her back to the door, and she was looking through a notebook.

Nathan signaled to Scott, the bartender, to stay quiet as he approached her. When he was behind her, he reached around with the flowers, holding them in front of her.

The move startled her at first, but then she turned around and saw Nathan. "What's this for?"

"I had to find some way to apologize to you for this morning. Can I join you?"

"Of course." She took the flowers and placed them on the table.

Nathan looked toward the bar. "Scott, can you bring me a draft?" The bartender nodded and Nathan sat down.

"I'm sorry about the way I talked to you this morning. I should have known that you wouldn't write about my injuries after you said you wouldn't."

"Apology accepted. I talked to my editor after I left you this morning. He admitted that he had rewritten my article."

"How did he find out about my time in the army?"

"He's a newspaper man. He has connections all over."

Scott sat Nathan's beer in front of him on the table. "Can I get either of you anything else? More iced tea, Miss Tyler, or maybe some menus?"

"Nothing for me," she said, looking at Nathan.

"Nothing for me either. Thanks, Scott." Nathan looked at Dana. "Iced tea?"

"I have to cover the school board meeting later. I hope that article didn't cause you too much trouble." She took a sip through the straw of her tea.

"Not much. The guys at work didn't want me to sign up for the department softball team because of it, but I did anyway. If the other teams remember that article when the season starts, I just might be our team's secret weapon."

"I'll look forward to a season of games then." She looked at her watch. "I should probably go. I want to change clothes at home before heading to the meeting." She put her notebook away and started to slide out of the booth.

"Wait." He reached over and grabbed her hand. "I need to ask you something before you go."

She stopped.

"I have two tickets to the dinner theater tomorrow night downtown. Would you like to go with me?"

"That sounds like fun. Yes, I'd love to go. What time

should I be ready?"

It suddenly occurred to him that he didn't know what time it started. He reached into his pocket and pulled out the tickets. "Dinner is at seven. How does six-fifteen sound? That should give us plenty of time to get there and be seated."

Six-fifteen sounds fine. I'll see you then." She slid out of the booth and picked up her flowers. "Thanks again for the flowers. They're beautiful."

Chapter Nine

Saturday morning

The ringing of Nathan's phone awakened him at seven o'clock. He reached over and grabbed his cell phone. "Hello."

"Detective Perry, I hope I'm not calling too early."

"Who is this?" Nathan pulled himself upright on the bed.

"It's Ryan Avery. I woke you up. I'm so sorry, sir. I can call back later."

"Ryan, wait. What do you want?"

"I found the car that drove by the Newcomb's house that morning."

"Who was it?" Nathan swung his legs over and sat on the side of the bed, rubbing his injured leg. He could usually tell if the weather was changing by the way it felt.

"It was Marc Mahoney and he said he saw an older model black pickup truck parked on the street."

"Mahoney? Why do I know that name?"

"His father is Quentin Mahoney, head of the Homeowners' Association on the island."

"That's right. He didn't know the make or model?"

"No, sir. Only that it was a black pickup."

"Are you working today, Ryan?"

"Yes, sir."

"Could you call and have Marc Mahoney and his father come down to the department around one-o'clock? I'd like to talk to the boy myself."

"Yes, sir. I'll call them right now."

"Thanks. I'll see you then." Nathan hung up the phone and stood. He limped to the bathroom. His mornings usually started out with a limp and the more he moved, the sooner the limp went away.

After he dressed, he went into the kitchen and looked in the refrigerator, trying to decide what to have for breakfast. It looked pretty bare in there with half a dozen eggs, an empty carton of milk, some cheese, and a few bottles of beer. "I really need to get to the grocery store." He heard a knock at the kitchen door and then it opened.

"Good morning," Ginger said, walking into the house. She carried a brown paper bag that she sat on the counter.

"Good morning to you too."

"I thought I'd get an early start on cleaning today. I hope you don't mind."

"That's fine, but I thought you were going to on Friday's while I was at work."

"I was, but I got busy yesterday. Here, this might help your morning go better." She handed him a large cup of coffee from the bag she carried in.

"That's exactly what I need." He removed the lid off and took a sniff before taking a drink. "You have the best coffee in town, Ginger."

"What are you having for breakfast?" she asked, opening up the refrigerator. "Lord, have mercy. You don't have any food."

"What do you mean? I have eggs and cheese. I could make an omelet," he boasted.

Ginger laughed and then handed him a Styrofoam container from the bag. It was warm, and when he opened it, he found biscuits and gravy. "Here's your newspaper. I got it out of your box when I pulled in the driveway."

"You're going to spoil me, if you keep bringing food and coffee to me."

"Don't worry. I'm running you a tab at the café," she winked. She then got the broom and dustpan out of the closet and headed to the bathroom to start cleaning.

Nathan sat down at the kitchen table to eat his breakfast and read the newspaper.

That afternoon, Nathan walked into the police department and found Officer Avery waiting for him next to his office. "Good afternoon, Ryan. Are the Mahoney's here?"

"Yes, sir. They're waiting in the lobby. Mr. Mahoney was none too happy about having to come in here today and his son was even worse about it."

"I'm not surprised." Nathan unlocked his office door and went inside, followed by Ryan. "Go ahead and take them to interrogation room one and I'll be right in."

"Yes, sir."

Avery left and Nathan hung his coat on the wall hook and then got a file out of the desk drawer, along with a pad of paper and pen. He saw Avery and the Mahoney's walk past his office. He went out and followed them.

With everyone seated in the interrogation room, Nathan began. "Thank you for bringing your son in today, Mr. Mahoney. I had a few follow-up questions for Marc about the truck he saw in front of the Newcomb's home Monday morning."

"I already told him what I saw," Marc Mahoney said, nodding toward Ryan.

"As I said, I have a few follow-up questions. Can you tell me what the make and model of the truck was you saw?" Nathan asked.

"Like I said, I already said I didn't know."

"What kind of car do you have, Marc?" Nathan asked.

"My car?" The teenager smiled. " I have a brand, new Ford Mustang with 5.0-liter Tri VCT V8 engine."

"What about the police car that Officer Avery here

drives?"

Marc looked at Avery. He drives an old Dodge Charger. It's a piece of shit."

"Watch your mouth," his father ordered.

Nathan hid a chuckle. "I can't imagine you didn't notice a truck like that sitting on the street."

"A truck like that? Piece of shit is what it was."

"Marc." Mr. Mahoney stopped his son from speaking any more.

"So, you're telling me that you know the make and model of Officer Avery's car that you only see occasionally and everything about your own car, but all you noticed about that truck was that it's a piece of shit? I don't buy it, Marc."

The younger Mahoney looked at his father for help.

"If you know something, son, you better tell them or you'll suffer the consequences when you get home."

The boy lowered his head, looking at the table where he sat. "It was a 1976 blue and white Chevy Silverado pickup truck. The sides were all rusted out because, you know, that was a bad year for Chevy trucks."

Nathan looked at Ryan, who was smiling, and then back at the Mahoney boy. "Thank you, Marc. I appreciate you sharing that information."

"That guy you're looking for. Will he know that I told you about his truck?"

"Probably not. If we can locate him, Mrs. Newcomb can identify him. There shouldn't be any need to involve you further, unless you know who he is?"

"No, I have no idea and I didn't see him either," the boy quickly replied.

"I think we're all finished then. You can go home. Thanks for coming in," Nathan said.

Mr. Mahoney and his son got up and left the room without saying another word.

"Do you think he told us everything he knows?" Ryan asked.

"I doubt it, but it's all we were going to get from him today."

"If that's all you need from me, I should probably get back on patrol."

"Sure, go ahead. Thanks for your help, Ryan."

After Avery left the room, Nathan walked back to his office. He put everything back where he got it from earlier, got his coat from the hook, and locked his office door on the way out. He had to go home to get ready for his date.

When he arrived at his house, Ginger was in the kitchen, getting ready to leave. She looked up when he walked in. "That was fast," she said.

"I just had to interview a kid. I brought food home, if you're hungry."

"You brought food for me? Where did you get it?"

"I stopped by Capt's Waterfront Bar and Grill for a couple sandwiches and some fries. Anything wrong with that?"

She laughed. "Nope. Let's see what you got?"

He put the sack on the counter. Ginger opened it and got the sandwiches and fries out. Nathan got a couple bottles of water out of the refrigerator and they sat down for lunch.

"So, who did you interrogate, or is that classified?" she asked.

Nathan chuckled. "I didn't actually interrogate anyone. I just had some follow-up questions for Marc Mahoney."

"Quentin Mahoney's kid? I bet daddy wasn't any too happy about that."

"He wasn't."

"He's always walking around like he's all high and mighty. He won't even come into my place cause it isn't good enough for his sorry ass," Ginger said.

"I'm sure that isn't true."

"It is. Dana wanted to interview him when he was elected head of the Homeowners' Association and asked him to meet her there. He told her he'd prefer a higher-class establishment."

"What did Dana do when he said that?"

"She told him it was my place or no interview."

"So, there was no interview, right?"

"There wasn't until her editor made her meet him somewhere else."

"Her editor's a real piece of work, isn't he?"

"He's been in the café a few times. He wants things done his way or else, but that's what makes the newspaper as good as it is. It's won several awards."

Nathan was starting to feel even more guilty about his argument with Dana over the article. "Dana told me she didn't write about my injures. I guess she was right. I had my ex-girlfriend do some checking at the hospital where I was. Someone did call and asked about my injuries. The girl in the Records Department told Katherine she didn't release any information, but I have a feeling she did. I bet it was Dana's editor."

"If her editor knew about it and she didn't write about it, he would see to it that it was added. Did you apologize to her?"

"I did and gave her flowers."

"After seeing your argument with her on the sidewalk, you need to do more." She got up to toss her lunch wrapper into the garbage can.

Nathan got up to do the same. "I'm taking her to the dinner theater in town tonight."

"What's your relationship with her?" Ginger asked.

"That's a little personal, isn't it?" He leaned back against the counter.

"Do you want my advice, or not?" She picked up the dust mop and other cleaning supplies next to the table and put them into the kitchen closet.

"I'm not trying to have a romantic relationship with her. It's just nice to have some companionship once in a while." He was very uncomfortable talking about this with Ginger.

"Dinner and theater tonight should be enough, but you

need to make sure she knows that your relationship is not going to lead anywhere, unless you think it will."

"I have no immediate plans for that. She and I have talked about it. She understands."

"Just make sure she does. I don't want to see that girl hurt. She's a good friend."

"I won't hurt her." Nathan said.

"Good." Ginger got her coat from the chair and put it on. "I'll be back next week. Don't forget to take your laundry out of the dryer soon."

"Thanks, Ginger. I won't forget."

"Drop my payment off at the café tomorrow." She stepped out the door and left.

Ginger was right. He needed to make sure he wasn't giving Dana the wrong idea. It's nice knowing she'd likely be available for a date when he wanted to go out, but not a steady thing. His job would take up a majority of his time and it wouldn't be fair to her.

That evening, he arrived right on time to pick Dana up for the theater. He knocked on her door and waited.

It didn't take long for her to answer. "Good evening, Nathan."

Dressed in a little black dress with a strand of pearls around her neck, she took his breath away. "Good evening. You look beautiful." He leaned down and gave her a peck on the cheek.

"Would you like to come in?"

He looked at his watch. "We probably should get going. I don't want to be late."

"Of course, let me get my coat."

Nathan stepped in and helped her on with her coat and then walked her to his truck. He helped her step up into it since it was a little difficult to do in her dress and heels. He closed the door and went around to the driver's side and got in. He started the engine and drove off.

"You look really good tonight too and I love the scent of

your aftershave."

"Thanks. Have you ever been to one of their dinner theaters before?" he asked.

"I attended their first one to do a review of the play. The food was really good, the play, not so much."

"That doesn't sound good."

"But, that was several years ago and all the actors have changed since. I'm sure they're better now."

"Let's hope."

"How is your job working out? Has Chief Cabot made you permanent yet?" she asked.

"The way things are going, I might need to start looking through the employment ads soon."

"That bad?"

"Investigations tend to take time and the chief doesn't seem to remember that. How long has he been chief?"

"You don't know?"

"Know what?"

The chief of police position is a political appointment. They work at the pleasure of the mayor. Most of the past mayors never changed the police chief, but when Robert Newcomb came into office, he appointed Chief Cabot. The former chief was demoted to captain and eventually just retired."

"But, he was a police officer when he was appointed, right?"

"Yes, he was a patrol officer. The oldest one on the force," Dana said.

"Wait, you mean he went from being a patrol officer to chief of police without any other experience?"

"Believe me, the whole town went into shock when Newcomb appointed him."

"I'll bet. What did Newcomb do before becoming mayor?"

"He worked as the Chief Financial Officer at Boston General Hospital."

Nathan laughed. "He left a job that probably paid him six figures to become mayor in Mystic, Massachusetts? That doesn't make any sense."

"Apparently, he's got money and didn't need to stay at the CFO job."

"Why are you so interested in the chief and the mayor?" she asked.

"It looks more and more each day that I need to play the political game in order to get and keep my job. I need to keep up to date on my superiors."

Nathan turned his truck into the parking lot next to the theater and shut off the motor. He got out and walked around to open Dana's door and help her out. As they walked toward the theater door, he put his hand at the small of her back.

A crowd was at the door, entering one at a time. Nathan held the door for Dana and then handed the usher their tickets once inside. Looking at their tickets, and then at the seating chart, the usher said, "You'll be at table number seven. It's through those doors and to the left."

"Thanks," Nathan said.

Dana checked her coat at the rear of the theater, and then she and Nathan found their table. He held her chair while she sat down. They were the first at their table. The theater was set up with round tables covered with white tablecloths. With six chairs to each table, the silverware, water goblets, and coffee cups were already in place.

Nathan took his seat next to Dana. "This isn't a bad table. We're not in the center where everyone can see us, but we can still see the stage with no problem. I like this."

That feeling didn't last long as another couple arrived at the table. "Detective Perry, I didn't know you liked the theater." It was Mayor Newcomb and his wife.

Nathan stood as the mayor helped his wife sit and then took his seat, and then Nathan returned to his chair. "It's not something I do often, but I did attend a few plays in D.C. while I lived there."

"Detective, I want to thank you again for coming to the house to check on me after that horrible man tried to get into my home," Mrs. Newcomb said.

"It's all in a day's work, ma'am. Do you know my date, Dana Tyler?"

"Yes, I do," the mayor said. "Honey, Miss Tyler is a reporter at the newspaper in town."

"I've read your stories. You're very good," Mrs. Newcomb said.

"Thank you," Dana replied.

The third couple arrived at the table, John Hawkins and his wife. Both Nathan and the mayor stood until Mrs. Hawkins was seated. "It looks like we're in good company tonight. It's good to see you, Mr. Mayor, Mrs. Newcomb," Hawkins said.

"John, have you met our new police detective?" Mayor Newcomb asked.

"Yes, I have. He stopped by the office the other day. Detective, this is my wife, Mary. Dear, you know Dana, right?"

"I do. How have you been, Dana?"

"Very well. It's nice seeing you again."

A waiter approached the table. "Good evening." He took a deep bow. "I'm Charles and I'll be your waiter tonight until the show starts and then I become the brother of the murder victim." They all laughed as he handed each of them a menu. "These are the food choices tonight. Can I take your drink orders first?"

Everyone ordered a cocktail, and he left to fetch their drinks.

"Detective, did you find anything on the video from City Hall?" Hawkins asked.

"Now, John," the mayor said. "Let's let the detective have a night off from work tonight."

"Of course." Hawkins looked at Nathan. "My apologies."

"It's okay. We're still looking into a few things. Our technician is still evaluating each frame to see if she can find anything usable."

"That's fascinating," Mrs. Hawkins said. "It's just like one of those C.S.I. shows, isn't it?"

"Well, there's a little more to it than it appears on television. It's long tedious work and I'll owe our technician a bouquet of flowers after all the long hours she'll spend on this."

"I wasn't aware that we had a technician with such training," Newcomb said.

"She studied forensics at Salem State College."

The waiter returned with their drinks, took their food orders, and then left.

"Detective, what about Raymond Miller's murder investigation? Any closer to finding who did it?" Hawkins asked.

Nathan smiled at Dana and then back at Hawkins. "You forget I'm here with a member of the press. I'm not sure I should be revealing information about an ongoing investigation right now."

The crowd at the table laughed. "I suppose you're right," Hawkins replied.

"Speaking of the local media, I read the article about you in the newspaper and was surprised to learn about your injuries from Afghanistan," the mayor said. "I hope your condition has improved enough to handle your duties at your job."

Mrs. Newcomb touched her husband's arm. "Dear, you promised no work talk tonight either."

"Of course. I'm sorry, detective."

"No need to apologize. The article, that actually wasn't written by Miss Tyler, exaggerated my injuries. I've recovered quite well and passed the department's physical exam."

After they received and finished their dinner, the waiters cleared the dishes from the table and took their final drink orders. Soon, the lights dimmed and the play began.

Once it was over, the other patrons in the room stood to leave. Everyone except the group at Nathan's table, who stayed in their seats. Apparently, they all had the same idea of letting the crowd thin before leaving.

"That was a very good performance," Nathan said.

"I wouldn't have expected any less," the mayor replied.

"I've never been to a community theater performance before, so I wasn't sure what to expect." Nathan felt like he had put his foot in his mouth and was trying to make up for it.

"I think it was one of their best," Mrs. Newcomb said.

"Detective, you should purchase season tickets from the theater. I can see to it that you'll be at our table for each performance," Mayor Newcomb suggested.

Nathan squirmed in his seat. "Well sir, unless you can make my job permanent and give me a pay raise, I think I'll have to stick with only occasional productions."

The mayor laughed. "I suppose you're right." He stood and helped his wife stand. "I think we should be going? John, drinks at O'Shea's tonight?"

"Wonderful idea. Detective, would you and Miss Tyler like to join us for after theater drinks?"

"Thank you, but no. Maybe another time." Nathan held Dana's chair as she got up.

"It's was wonderful having dinner with all of you," Dana said, looking at everyone. "Have a nice evening."

"Drive safe," the mayor said.

Nathan and Dana went to get her wrap from the coat check. "You didn't want to have drinks with the mayor?" Dana teased.

"Not really." He handed the lady the receipt for their coats. "Tonight, was a bit too uncomfortable for me."

"Why?"

He took their coats and helped Dana on with hers. "Let's talk about it on the ride home."

Once they were in Nathan's truck, Dana returned to their previous conversation. "Why was tonight uncomfortable for you?"

"Don't you think it was a little strange that we were

seated with two of the most influential couples in town?"

"No, I don't. You were randomly given the tickets you purchased, right?"

"Well, yes."

"You've been in the newspaper lately, so you're better known in the community. And, I'd like to think that being with the top newspaper reporter in town might have something to do with it," she teased.

"But, the theater manager didn't know who I was bringing with me when I got the tickets."

"Okay, you got me on that one."

"What did you think of the mayor asking me about my injuries?"

"I didn't think anything about it."

"What about now? What do you think now that I've brought it up?"

Dana thought for a few seconds. "I suppose he could have wondered why Chief Cabot hadn't told him about it and if it could hamper you on the job. I think that's what everyone is thinking, don't you?"

"You're probably right, but I would have thought that the mayor would already know about my medical history. I would have expected Chief Cabot to have told him."

"You're still concerned over what the mayor and John Hawkins asked you about your investigations, aren't you?"

Nathan laughed, trying to brush it off. "No, I'm sure they were just being curious."

They reached Dana's home and Nathan shut the truck off and went around to help Dana down from his truck. He walked her to the door.

"Would you like to come in for a while?" she asked.

He looked at the door and then at Dana. "I think I need to take a rain-check tonight. I had an early morning call and I'm a little tired. I hope you don't mind."

"Not at all. I'm a little tired myself."

Nathan leaned down and gave her a kiss on the cheek.

"I'll call you next week."

"Goodnight, Nathan."

He watched as she opened her front door and went inside. When he heard her lock the door, he went back to his truck and drove home.

Chapter Ten

"**D**etective Perry? Are you busy?"

Nathan looked up to see Malory standing at his office door. "Not too busy. Please come in. How is your Monday morning going?"

Mallory entered and sat in front of his desk. "It's been busy. I have the still prints from the bank ATM video." She handed him the photos.

He looked through each black and white eight-by-ten photo. "They're a little blurry."

"It's hard to get sharp stills from a video. I tried to clean them up as best I could. Just about the only thing they're good for was to get the height of the subject, which I already emailed you about."

"At least we have that. Would it offend you if I had the State Police forensics lab take a shot at cleaning them up a little more?"

"Not at all. Their equipment is so much better than ours."

"Thanks."

"I have something else."

"Yes."

"The State Police said the partial palm print from the newspaper office wasn't enough for a match in their database. However, if you can get a full palm print from a suspect, they likely could either match it or use it to rule someone out."

"Good."

Suddenly Hank walked into Nathan's office. "There was another burglary on Mano Island last night. Officer Avery is already on the scene and I'm heading out there now. Want to come?"

"I do." Nathan stood. "Mallory, can you follow us out there and collect whatever evidence there might be?"

"Yes. I just need to get my case." She got up and left the office.

Nathan and Hank arrived at the scene and saw Officer Avery standing in the yard talking to a man and woman. Also standing around in the yard were several other people; likely neighbors wanting to know what was going on. Nathan instructed a couple of the other officers standing on the sidewalk to clear the yard of the people and keep them off the lawn.

Avery took notice when they walked up. "Detective Perry, Officer McCoy, this is Mr. and Mrs. Adams. It was their house that was broken into."

"Mr. and Mrs. Adams, I'm Detective Perry. I'm sorry to have to meet you under these circumstances."

"Thank you," Mr. Adams replied.

"Have you determined what's missing yet?"

"We made a list last night after the police left. We were so upset about it, we couldn't sleep," Mrs. Adams said.

"This is the list." Avery handed a sheet of paper to Nathan.

"It looks like everything they took is similar to the other burglaries. They took your laptop?"

"Yes," Mr. Adams answered. "Oh my God! I do my online banking with that laptop."

"Oh dear," Mrs. Adams gasped.

"I've got to go call the bank right now," her husband said. He turned and rushed into the house.

Mrs. Adams started to follow, but Nathan stopped her. "Mrs. Adams, one more question. Do you have a dog?"

"No, we don't."

"Thank you." Nathan heard a car stop near the house and turned to see Mallory getting out of the vehicle with her crime scene case.

"Where do you need me to start?" she asked Nathan, who looked to Officer Avery.

"They broke in through the back door, but the Adams' have been all through the house taking inventory. I'm not sure how much you will be able to get," Avery said.

"We won't know until we try," Mallory said. "Are the Adams' in the house? I'll need to take their prints to rule them out."

"They are on the phone with their bank right now. Ryan will you stay with Mallory until she's finished?" Nathan asked the officer.

"Yes, sir. I will." Avery led the way into the house with Mallory following.

"Detective Perry, Detective Perry!"

Nathan turned to see Mayor Newcomb being detained by the two officers. "You can let him through," Nathan called to them.

The mayor rushed up to Nathan and Hank. "Was anyone hurt?"

It was apparent to Nathan that the mayor was truly concerned. "No, no one was hurt."

"Thank God. Can I speak with the homeowners? I'd like to assure them that everything will be done to recover their items and find who did this."

"You can't enter the house until our technician is finished gathering evidence," Hank said.

"I know enough not to touch anything. I don't see why I can't go in there. I am the mayor, after all."

"As soon as Mallory has finished going over everything in the house, you can go in," Nathan said. "Until then, I'm afraid you'll need to wait at the sidewalk with everyone else."

"You're kidding, right?"

"No, sir. I'm not. It's standard operating procedure. No one, except police personnel, is allowed inside of the crime scene until we're finished."

He stared at Nathan. "This isn't over." He marched back to the sidewalk and pulled out his cell phone to make a call.

"You know he's calling the chief, don't you?"

Nathan let out a deep breath and scratched the back of his neck. "Yeah. I'm sure the chief will want to see me when I get back to the office."

"Actually, I think the chief is in Boston for a meeting or something today," Hank said.

"Well, that'll delay the inevitable for a while." Both men laughed. "I need to head back to the station. I have a hunch I want to check on. Can you stay here to keep the mayor out of the house until Mallory is finished?"

"Sure. What's the hunch?"

"I'll let you know as soon as I figure it out." Nathan got in his car and drove off. He hoped Hank could handle the mayor at the scene.

Back at the station, Nathan looked through the files of the burglary cases for the list of items that were stolen. "How about that."

"How about what?" Joe Cassidy stood at Nathan's office door.

"Nothing, nothing at all. What can I do for you, Joe?"

Cassidy entered the office and sat down. "I heard there was another burglary last night."

"There was. On Mano Island again. Same as the others." Nathan wasn't ready to share his hunch, especially with Joe Cassidy.

"Can you give me a little more than that?"

"The officers are still at the scene. I don't have anything to give you yet. Once I have something, I'll email it to you." Nathan stood, hoping Cassidy would get the hint. Apparently, he did as he stood also.

"I'd appreciate that." He started to leave, but Nathan

stopped him.

"Joe, how did you hear about the burglary?"

"The mayor called me. Have a good day." Cassidy turned and left the office.

Nathan sat back down at his desk and picked up the phone. He looked in a file and then dialed a number, tapping his pen on the desk, waiting for the recipient to answer.

"Hello."

"Mrs. Miller, this is Dective Perry. How are you today?"

"I'm fine, detective. Have you learned something about my husband's murder?"

"Not exactly. I do have a couple more questions though. Did the laptop that was stolen belong to your husband or did it belong to his company?"

"It was our personal laptop" she replied.

Did your husband use it to do his online banking?"

"Yes, we both used it for that, but we always logged out of our account."

"What about the accounting from the theater or his other clients?"

"He didn't keep any of client records on that computer, but sometimes he would use the laptop to access the files on the server at his office. Do you think they were after his records?"

"They could have been. Is there someone at his accounting office that I could talk to about their records?"

"Phillip Turner was his business partner. He should be able to answer any questions you have."

Thank you, Mrs. Miller." Nathan hung up the phone and then picked it up again to make another call. Again finding the number in the file, he dialed, but not to Miller's accounting office yet.

"Mystic Theater Company. This is Floyd Parker, can I help you?"

"Mr. Parker, this is Detective Perry. I have a couple additional questions, if you have the time."

"Certainly, detective. What do you need to know?"

Nathan sat up closer to his desk, ready to scribble some notes. "Did Mr. Miller use one of your computers when he worked on the accounting for the theater?"

"No, he didn't. He brought his own laptop and used it. I believe he logged onto our WiFi when he was here though."

"Have you checked the theater's bank account since his death?"

"No, I just recently hired Raymond's accounting firm to handle all of our finances. Raymond had been doing it pro bono, but his partner didn't like him to do that. He said something about needing to be under his proof of performance insurance."

Nathan jotted some notes. "So, as far as you know, his partner hasn't looked at the bank account yet?"

"I doubt it."

"Do you have access to look at your bank account online?"

"Yes."

"Could you do that while I wait? I want to make sure everything looks correct to you."

"Of course. Give me a few minutes to log in."

Nathan could hear Parker typing on the computer. "What? I don't understand this."

"What is it?"

"There's no money. It's gone. It looks like it was all withdrawn just this week," the manager said.

"How much money was taken?"

"We're a small theater group, but it was thousands. What am I going to do? I have charges coming in on that account."

"Mr. Parker, I'm going to send an officer down to take your report of the theft. In the meantime, you need to contact the bank and report this right away. They can tell you more about what to do."

"Yes. Thank you, Detective Perry."

Nathan hung up his phone and sat back in his chair.

He felt sorry for the theater manager but knew the Mystic community would do everything they could to help the theater get back on its feet.

He had one more call to make and dialed the next number.

"Turner and Miller Accountants, can I help you?" a lady said.

"This is Detective Nathan Perry from the Mystic Police Department. Can I speak with Phillip Turner?"

"One moment, please."

"Detective Perry, this is Phillip Turner. What can I do for you?"

"Mr. Turner, I have a few questions pertaining to Raymond Miller's death, if you have time."

"Of course, I'd be happy to help. Raymond was just a good person. I hope you can find the person who murdered him."

"We're doing our best. Mrs. Miller said the laptop her husband had with him and that was taken was their personal laptop, but he used it to access company files from home. Were you aware of that?"

"Yes, Raymond and I both work from home sometimes and use our personal computers for that. However, we never store files on our own laptops."

"Have you noticed any unusual activity on any of your accounts since his death?"

Turner hesitated before answering. "I haven't noticed anything, but I also haven't specifically been looking either."

"I'd appreciate it if you could check and get back to me. The manager at the Mystic Theater Company discovered that their bank account has been cleaned out."

"What! They're not trying to blame my company for that, are they?"

"I don't really know, but Mr. Miller apparently did use his laptop when he worked on their accounts," Nathan replied.

"I've got to call my lawyer right now."

"Of course. Thank you, Mr. Turner and please get back with me about your other accounts."

Nathan didn't know if his last comment was heard or not because Turner had already hung up the phone.

Chapter Eleven

Nathan sat studying the case files spread across his desk. He rubbed his forehead; he was missing something.

"Are we interrupting?" a female voice said from the door.

He looked up to see Mallory and Hank standing there. "No. Come in."

"We wanted to give you an update," Mallory said. They came into the office.

Hank sat down, but Mallory remained standing. "I need to get back to my office, but I wanted to let you know just from eyeballing the prints, they all looked to belong to the homeowners. I'm still going to run them, but don't get your hopes up."

"Thanks, Mallory."

"I'll let you know what I find." She turned and left the office.

Nathan's attention turned to Hank. "What happened after I left?"

"He was on the phone most of the time. When we finished up, he told me to let you know that one of his calls was to the chief and another was to Joe Cassidy. I'm sure both will be in touch with you."

"Cassidy has already been here. I'm still waiting on the chief's call," Nathan said.

"The mayor also went inside to talk to the homeowners

as soon as we were finished with the scene. Oh, Officer Avery said he would email his report to you as soon as he got it written up. Mr. Adams called his bank about their accounts and so far there's been no activity, but the bank is keeping an eye on it."

"Good. I'm anxious to see if there's an attempt to hack their accounts."

"When you left the scene, you said you had a hunch about something, what was it?"

"When I left there, I came back here to make some calls. Mrs. Miller said her husband used his laptop to work on the theater's accounting and also some other clients' accounts when he worked from home. I then called the theater manager and had him check their bank account. It had been cleaned out."

"You think the burglars were after laptops to access the victims' bank accounts?" Hank asked.

"I do. I also called Miller's business partner and he's checking with their clients to see if any of their accounts may have been accessed."

"And?"

"He didn't know. He said he'd check with his clients and get back to me."

"So, we're looking at a cyber crime. That's a new one for Mystic," Hank said.

"I think this is too much for Mallory to handle. Not that I don't think she's competent, but I'm going to ask her to coordinate with the State Police Cyber Crime unit to see if they can dig something up."

"She'll like working with them."

Nathan's phone rang. "Perry," he answered.

"This is Chief Cabot, I need you in my office, now."

He looked at Hank. "Yes, sir. I'll be right up." He hung up the phone. "The chief wants to see me, now," Nathan said, mocking the chief. " I suppose the mayor called him about not being allowed inside the crime scene earlier."

"Good luck with that." Hank left the office.

Nathan headed to the chief's office, taking the elevator today. He rounded the corner and knocked on the door.

"Come in."

Nathan walked in. half-expecting to see the mayor sitting there, but it was only Chief Cabot. "What can I do for you, chief?"

"Sit down, Perry." Nathan did just that. "The mayor called me earlier saying that he was denied access to speak to the homeowners of another burglary on Mano Island. Is that true?"

"Yes, it is. Evidence Technician Duncan was still inside the home with the owners taking their fingerprints and processing the crime scene. The mayor would only have been in the way of the evidence gathering and possibly contaminate the scene. This was explained to him outside the home."

"Detective Perry."

"Sir, if I could finish. I would have thought he would want everything done per standard operating procedure in order to expedite the solving of these burglaries on Mano Island. Honestly, I hope you will back me up on this with Mayor Newcomb."

"There's only so much I can do, Perry. I work at the pleasure of the mayor and you work for me. I don't like ruffling feathers and you need to remember that. If something like this happens again, it could cost you your job here."

"Yes, sir. I understand." Nathan was pissed that the chief was holding his job over his head like that. He hated playing politics but understood sometimes the job calls for it. "If that's all you need---"

"I want an update on your case. Are you any closer to finding who committed the murder?"

"I realize Mystic hasn't had a murder investigation for quite a while, but cases like this take time. I don't have any specific suspects, but I am waiting for some more information to come in."

"Did you contact the State Police for help and have you been working with Joe Cassidy on it?"

"I've been in contact with Detective Denzinger with the State Police and they have helped with some evidence. I actually spoke with Cassidy right after I got back from the scene of today's burglary." Technically, he told the truth about Cassidy. He needed the chief off his butt so he could concentrate on the case.

"Very well. Make sure you keep me updated. The mayor has asked me for any updates as well."

"I will. Thank you, sir." Nathan stood and left the office. He took the stairs back down to the first floor and was walking down the hallway to his office when a uniformed officer with a dog stopped him.

"Detective Perry, Sergeant Donnelly said you wanted to see me."

"You're Officer Riley?"

"Yes, sir and this is Dexter." The dog looked like he went to attention at the sound of his name.

"Please come into my office," Nathan said.

Both officers sat down. "What can I do for you, detective?"

"Dexter is a drug dog, right?"

"Yes, sir. One of the best."

"Are you familiar with a teenager named Marc Mahoney? He lives on Mano Island."

"I am. That's one spoiled kid."

"Sounds like you know him."

"Most of the patrol officers know him. You're wanting Dexter for Marc?"

"Yes. I questioned him the other day about the owner of a vehicle that may be the person that scared the mayor's wife and I don't think he was totally forthcoming with everything he knows. I'm guessing a drug dog circling his car might persuade his memory," Nathan said.

"When do you want to do this?"

Nathan looked at his watch. "School gets out in about thirty minutes, let's go wait for him at the bridge to Mano Island."

"What about probable cause?" Officer Riley asked.

"I don't plan on arresting him if we find something. I just want him to give me the info. Anything we find will be confiscated and destroyed. If it's something more than pot, I'll have a talk with his father."

"Dexter and I are ready." Dexter sat up at attention.

****

Gloria drove the patrol car onto Mano Island and, after passing a few streets, stopped in front of a large Colonial-style home. She hoped this worked out or the chief would probably have her badge. She went to the door and rang the bell. After what seemed like a long wait, the door finally opened.

"Yes, can I help you?" the little blue-haired lady asked.

"Mrs. Carson, I'm Officer Wheeler. We've spoken a few times over the phone and also in person at the police department."

Mrs. Carson looked confused.

"It was about the children that were bothering your house," Gloria reminded her.

You could almost see her memory kick in. "Oh, of course I remember you. Please come in." Mrs. Carson led Gloria to the living room where they both sat down. "Would you like some tea?" she offered.

"No, thank you. Not this time. I was wondering if you were still having problems with the children?"

"You know, I talked to that nice Quentin Mahoney about the problem and he said he'd say something to the parents on the island at the Homeowners Association meeting. He must have done that because the children haven't been bothering me as much. Are you sure you won't have some tea?"

"I think I would like some after all," Gloria said. The lady seemed desperate for company.

"Wonderful, I'll go fix it."

"Let me help." Gloria followed Mrs. Carson into the kitchen.

"Would you be a dear and get the sugar out of the cabinet over there?"

Gloria wasn't sure which cabinet 'over there' meant, so she started opening a few to find the sugar. When she opened the second cabinet, she was shocked to see a computer monitor showing the view of Mrs. Carson's front yard from the porch. "What's this?"

"Oh honey, the sugar isn't in that cabinet. It's in the one next to it." She opened the other cabinet and got the sugar dish out.

"But, what is this monitor? Do you have a security system?"

"That's some kind of electronic thingy that my son put in. He told me not to open that cabinet." She walked over and closed the door that Gloria had opened. "The other part of it is in the hall closet. Do you want cream for your tea?"

"No. Thank you."

Mrs. Carson poured hot water into a tea pot on the tray and then placed the sugar dish on there too. "Here we are. Would you mind carrying this into the living room? I'm not as steady as I used to be."

"Of course." Gloria picked up the tray and took it to the table in front of the couch and sat it down. Mrs. Carson followed, and they both sat on the couch.

Gloria spooned some sugar into her tea and took a sip. "This is very good tea."

"Thank you. It's Earl Grey. My favorite." She added sugar and cream into her tea.

"Mrs. Carson, would you mind if I took a look at that---electronic thingy in your closet? As a police officer, I should check to make sure everything is okay with it and that it doesn't pose a hazard."

"Oh my, if you think there's something wrong, by all means, check it."

"I just want to make sure."

"It's right this way." Mrs. Carson led Gloria into a hallway and opened the closet door.

Inside, Gloria found a video surveillance system that rivaled the one the police department had monitoring their building. "How long have you had this?"

"My son put it in a few months ago, I think. Does it look okay?"

"Yes. Would you mind if I looked at the monitor in the cabinet again?"

"I don't see why not. You're a police officer."

The two ladies went back to the kitchen where Gloria opened the cabinet door to view the monitor. She wanted to see how much of the neighborhood was visible by the camera.

Once she was satisfied with what she had seen, she closed the door, and they went back to the living room. Gloria sat down and took another sip of her tea. "Could I have your son's phone number? I'd like to talk to him about your surveillance system."

"My what?"

"Your electronic thingy," Gloria said.

"Is there something wrong?"

Gloria was afraid she had frightened Mrs. Carson. "No, no, nothing's wrong. It's a very good system and I'd like to ask him where he purchased it."

"Well, I suppose it would be okay. He's on vacation with his family right now, so he won't be home for a few days."

"Do you have his cell phone number?"

"I only have one number for him. I'm sorry."

"That's okay. I'll take whatever number you have."

Mrs. Carson went to the beautiful Victorian era desk in the living room and looked through an address book. She finally wrote something down on a piece of paper and brought it over to Gloria. "Here you are. His name is Thomas, but he won't be home from vacation for two more days."

"Thank you, Mrs. Carson. If you speak with him, please tell him I'll be calling." Gloria stood to leave. "If you have any more trouble with the neighborhood children, make sure and give us a call at the police department."

"I will, honey. Thank you for stopping to check on me. I hope you can stay longer next time.

Gloria got back into her car and drove away. After crossing the bridge from Mano Island, she saw one of the Mystic police cars sitting on the side of the road. With no traffic coming, she pulled over next to the marked car and was surprised to see Nathan sitting with Officer Riley. "What are you guys doing here?"

"Riley and I are waiting for Marc Mahoney to drive by so we can stop him and let Dexter check his car," Nathan said. Dexter, who had been laying on the back seat, sat up at the sound of his name.

"Probable cause?" Gloria asked.

"We're just going to scare him," Riley said.

"I'm pretty sure he has some info on the truck that was at the mayor's house and he needs a little encouragement to tell us about it," Nathan added.

Gloria could see some traffic coming toward them. "I better go before I get hit. I may have some info for you myself soon." With that, she drove away.

A few cars drove by that looked like high school kids, but not the Mahoney boy. Finally, in the rearview mirror, Nathan saw a Mustang coming behind them. "I think that's him."

Sure enough Marc Mahoney slowly drove by. Officer Riley started the car and turned on the red and blue lights. Mahoney pulled over just after crossing the bridge and Riley pulled right behind him. Nathan got out. Riley got out but stayed next to the patrol car, with his dog inside.

Nathan approached the driver's window. "Hello, Marc. License and registration, please."

"I didn't do anything."

"License and registration, please," he repeated.

The teenager got his license out and dug the car registration from the glove compartment. He handed both to Nathan.

"Marc, do you have any drugs in your car?"

"What? No sir, I do not."

Nathan looked down at the kid. "Marc, I have a drug dog waiting to check your car. You want to try that again?"

"I don't have anything in the car. Maybe one of my friends smoked a joint in here this morning, but there's nothing in here now."

Nathan, being overly dramatic, shook his head. "Marc, Marc, Marc. One more time. Do you have any illegal substances in your possesssion or in the car?"

Mahoney hesitated. "No, I don't and I don't think you have the right to check my car. I didn't do anything wrong."

"Please step out of the car."

"No."

Nathan did a double-take. He couldn't believe the kid said no. "Listen, you'll either step out of the car under your own power or I'll pull you out through the window myself." The boy opened the door and slowly got out. "Good choice, now please walk back to the patrol car." He did as instructed and Nathan followed him. He nodded at Officer Riley. It was now the dog's turn.

Riley opened the door of the police car and attached the leash to Dexter's collar. The dog jumped out and tried to dash to the Mahoney car, nearly pulling Riley off his feet. "Dex, stop." The dog immediately stopped and sat next to Riley. Then, the officer took a step next to the car and motioned with his hand at the rear tire. "Dexter, search."

The dog went to the tire and excitedly started sniffing as Riley led him around the car. When they reached the driver side door, Dex instantly sat down.

"Marc, do you know what it means when a drug dog sits

down?" Nathan asked. The teenager didn't answer. "It means he has indicated the smell of drugs and we can now search your car."

Riley tossed Dex a rubber ball as reward and the dog jumped on it. He then brought Dexter over to where Nathan and Marc were standing.

"Stay here while I check the car," Nathan said to the officer. He walked over to the car and opened the driver door and reached under the seat, pulling out a plastic bag of what looked like pot. He looked back at the Mahoney boy, "I suppose this is oregano?"

Marc stood with his hands in his pockets. "So, you found my pot. What do you want?"

Nathan walked back to where Mahoney and the officer stood. "I want to know what you're not telling us about that truck you saw in front of the mayor's house. I think you know more than you admitted to."

He didn't answer, just stared down at the ground.

"Marc, you can tell me now and I'll let you go, or we can go down to the police department and I'll book you in as having a controlled substance."

"In case you forgot, because I know you haven't lived here in a while, pot's legal in Massachusetts."

"How old are you, Marc?" Nathan asked.

"Eighteen."

"You're old enough to know that the law says it's legal if you're twenty-one and have less than an ounce in your possession somewhere other than your home." Nathan held up the baggie of weed." I'd be willing to bet this is more than an ounce. What do you think, Officer Riley?"

"It looks like more than an ounce to me, but we should probably take it to the department to weigh it."

"Okay, okay. I'll tell you about the truck."

"Who owns it?"

"His name is Frank Bishop."

"Where does he live?"

"Last I knew, he lived in some shack on Forrester St."

"What about his work? Where does he work?" Nathan asked.

"I don't think he works anywhere."

"Well, that wasn't so bad now, was it? Thanks for your help, Marc. You can go."

"Hey, what about my pot?"

"This pot?" Nathan held up the baggie. "Oh, this is going to the police department for incineration."

"Seriously? You're going to burn it?"

"Isn't that what you were going to do with it? We're just doing it a different way." Nathan laughed as he, Riley, and Dexter got into the police car and left.

Back at the police department, Nathan and Riley entered the building by the rear door and Dexter followed. "Officer Riley, I really appreciate your and Dexter's help today."

"I'm glad to help, Detective. Just call if you need anything else," Riley said. He made a motion to the dog and they both turned and walked away.

Nathan went to the front desk to let them know he was back and to stop by the evidence room. Gloria sat at her station. "I'm back now, but only for a short time until I go home."

"Thanks," she said. "How'd it go?"

"We got the information we needed."

"That's great. The phone rang and as Gloria answered, he headed to see Mallory.

At the doorway to the evidence room, Nathan stopped at the locked door and knocked. "Good afternoon, Detective Perry," Mallory greeted.

"Please, call me Nathan."

"I'm not sure I can do that." She walked over to the chain link door. What can I do for you?"

He placed the plastic bag of marijuana on the shelf of the door. "I need you to log this in for incineration."

She pulled out a form and placed it on a clipboard. "Case

number?"

"No case number. I took it off of a kid and it just needs to be destroyed."

"I see." She jotted some things down on the form and handed it to him through the opening in the door. "Sign here."

He took the form and signed his name.

"We incinerate in two days," she said. Taking the clipboard back from him, she stamped something on the form, put the bag of pot into an evidence bag, and wrote something on it. "Thank you for your contribution."

"Thank you for taking it off my hands." Being close to the end of the day, Nathan was ready to head home. Before going, however, he went to his office to enter Frank Bishop' information into the computer so the department's officers would be on the lookout.

When Nathan returned to work the next morning, Gloria met him coming into the building. "Officer Avery needs to see you right away," she said, following him.

He reached his office and went inside, removing his coat and hanging it up. "What about?"

"He made an arrest this morning and he's waiting in Booking for you."

"Thanks, Gloria." Skipping his morning coffee for now, he heading to the booking room where he found Avery. "You needed to see me, Ryan?"

"Yes." He handed Nathan a booking document. "I arrested Frank Bishop this morning."

"That didn't take long. Good job."

"I thought you'd want to talk to him."

"I do. Can you have his mug shot emailed to me? I want to send it to the mayor's wife for identification."

"Yes, sir. He's waiting in room one."

Nathan went down the hallway and entered the interrogation room. Sitting at the table with his hands handcuffed to the top of the table was Bishop. "Good morning, Mr. Bishop. I'm glad you could join us here." Nathan's cell phone rang, indicating an email had been received. He looked at it and saw it was Bishop' mug shot.

"What am I doing here? What was I arrested for?" he asked.

Officer Riley stepped into the room and stood by the door. "Officer Riley, was Mr. Bishop read his rights?"

"Yes, sir. He was. I did it myself."

"Good. Would you stay here with him for a moment while I step out into the hallway to make a call?"

"Yes, sir."

Nathan stepped into the outer hallway, looked up a number from the file he carried, and dialed it on his phone. "Mrs. Newcomb, this is Detective Perry from the Mystic PD."

"Good morning, detective. What can I do for you?"

"I'd like to email you a photo to see if it's the person that was at your home trying to see your husband. Could you give me your email address?"

"Certainly." She gave him her address and he emailed the photo. "Oh, my goodness! That's him."

He could hear the nervousness in her voice. "We have him in custody. There's no need to worry."

"Thank you, detective. I appreciate you letting me know. If there's anything else I can do."

"I think you've done all I need for now. Did you get your new front door put in?"

"Yes, we did. Thank you for asking."

"Thank you for your help. Goodbye, Mrs. Newcomb." He ended the call and stepped back into the interrogation room. "Good news, Frank. We are going to supply you with three hot's and a cot." Bishop looked at Nathan confused. "You're going to be in jail for a while."

"For what!"

"You tried to gain entry into the mayor's home when his wife told you he wasn't there. You were also disturbing the peace at his office that same day. You better get yourself an attorney." Nathan turned to Avery. "Book him on illegal entry and disturbing the peace." He looked at Bishop. "And, that's just to start."

"Yes, sir."

Nathan left and went back to his office.

Chapter Twelve

That next morning, Mayor Newcomb sat at the dining room table eating breakfast as he powered up his laptop. The first thing that popped up was his wife's email account, and he saw an email from Nathan. "Brenda, what's this email from that police detective to you?" he called to his wife.

She walked in with her plate of eggs and fruit and sat at the table. "Oh, I was asleep when you got home last night from the board meeting so I couldn't tell you. The police arrested that man who tried to get into the house when you weren't here. The detective emailed me his picture so I could confirm it was him and it was. Open the email and look at the guy, if you want."

He opened the email and looked at the photo. "That's him, eh? I'll have to make sure and thank Detective Perry on some fine police work."

"Yes, you should. I can't tell you how much better I feel knowing that man is behind bars now."

****

At the police department, Nathan was going over the information on the sign burglaries when his phone rang. "Detective Perry."

"Perry, Chief Cabot here. Get up to my office right now." The chief hung up the phone before Nathan could respond.

"This can't be good," he said to himself. Opting for the stairs rather than the elevator, he reached the second floor in no time. He approached the chief's door and heard a familiar voice as he rounded the corner.

"Perry, get in here," the chief said. Inside with Chief Cabot was Mayor Newcomb.

Nathan entered the office and stood next to where the mayor sat. He didn't dare take the other seat unless instructed to by the chief.

The mayor spoke first. "Detective, my wife told me this morning that you've arrested the man that tried to force his way into my home. Who was it?"

"His name is Frank Bishop. He's a local guy with some priors for break-ins."

Newcomb stood to shake Nathan's hand. "I want to thank you for the arrest," Newcomb said.

"I'd like to take full credit for that, sir, but it was actually Officer Ryan Avery that made the arrest. I just gathered the information on the description of the man and his vehicle."

"The town of Mystic thanks both of you then. Chief, you have made a good choice in your new detective and I believe a certificate of commendation is due to Officer Avery." The mayor sat back down.

At first, the chief was speechless, but then found his voice. "I'll see that Officer Avery is given a certificate at tomorrow's roll call. In the meantime, Detective Perry still needs to solve the Mano Island murder before I make him a permanent member of the department, sir."

"I'm sure he will have that solved in no time," Newcomb said.

"Of course, he will. Perry, you can go now."

Nathan just stood there. "Mayor, did your wife show you the photo I emailed to her?"

"Yes, she did. Why?"

"It's my thought that Frank Bishop is also the same man that was trying to see you at your office that day. We've actually charged him with disturbing the peace for the incident at your office."

"So, you're sure it was him?" the mayor asked.

"We viewed the short clip of video available from the surveillance camera from outside of your office door. It's only a few seconds, but we believe it's the same man."

"Good work, Detective Perry."

"Thank you, sir." Nathan started to leave but stopped. "Sir, if I might make a suggestion. The camera in the hallway outside of your office isn't working. Both the security guard at City Hall and John Hawkins said there is a budget situation keeping it from being replaced. I think this should be a high priority, and it needs to be replaced as soon as possible."

"I think you're right. I'll see to it that the money is appropriated for it right away. Thank you."

Nathan nodded to the mayor and left the office.

Gloria was waiting for him at his office door. "Are you still employed?" She followed him into his office.

"Of course, I am. The mayor wanted to thank me for arresting the guy that tried to get into his house."

"Good. I've been doing some calling to those antique stores in Boston and I think I found some of the stolen signs."

"You did? That's fantastic. Did they have a description of the person that they bought them from?"

"They did, but it was a pretty general description. Tomorrow is my day off and I thought I might drive up there to talk to them in person."

"Working on your day off? Are you sure you want to do that?" he asked.

"It's the only way I would ever get to go. The chief would never let me go on work time. You wouldn't want to go with me, would you? It would make it more official."

"I really can't be away from the office that long. I've got to work on this murder case. I'm sorry."

"That's fine. I'll let you know what I come up with. I better get back up front.," she rushed out of the office.

He could tell she was disappointed, but the sign thefts just weren't a priority for him right now. He went back into his office and sat down. A few minutes later, Sam Denzinger from the State Police walked in.

"Busy?" Denzinger asked.

"Not for you. What are you doing here?"

Denzinger sat down. "You're chief called yesterday and asked me to stop by. He said he wanted to talk to me about a murder case that had gone cold. I assumed it was the Miller case."

"I'm not surprised. He's not been happy with my investigation of it."

"You've been emailing me updates. From what I read, I don't think I would do anything different."

"I hope you'll tell him that. He was with the mayor a few minutes ago, but they may be finished by now."

Denzinger looked at his watch. "I will most definitely tell him that. It's about time for my appointment with him. I better get up there." He stood to leave. "If you need anything, let me know."

"I will. Thanks."

Denzinger left.

Nathan's day didn't get any better. He spent the whole time going over the files for the Mano Island burglaries and the Miller murder. He knew there was something there. It had to be right in front of him, but he couldn't see it.

A correctional officer from the jail appeared at his doorway. "Detective, Frank Bishop's lawyer is ready for you to meet with her client now. They're in interrogation room one."

"Thanks. I'll be right there." Nathan pulled Bishop's file out of his desk drawer and walked down to the interrogation room. He entered to find Bishop and his attorney sitting on one side of the table.

"I'm Detective Perry." He extended his hand to the

attorney.

"I'm Christina Thompson, Frank's attorney." She handed him her card and then shook hands with Nathan. This was no run of the mill attorney. She wore a black skirt suit and had perfect makeup and not a blonde hair was out of place. She looked all business.

"You're not a public defender, are you?" Nathan asked.

"No, I'm with a firm out of Boston."

"How does a firm out of Boston come to represent someone like Frank here?" He looked at Bishop, who gave him a resentful look.

"We do pro bono work occasionally. This is one of them."

"I see."

"Can we get down to business, detective? I need to return to Boston to meet with other clients."

"You mean, paying clients? Of course." He sat down on the opposite side of the table and opened the file folder.

Before he could ask his first question, Ms. Thompson jumped in. "Just so you understand, I've advised my client not to answer any of your questions."

"It sounds like it's going to be a one-sided conversation then. Frank, why did you need to talk to the mayor so bad that day at his home? Did you want to confess something to him?"

Frank looked at his attorney, who shook her head.

"You know, you scared the hell out of his wife when you tried to force yourself into the home. Why would you want to intimidate her like that?"

Frank was fidgeting in his chair. He pursed his lips and Nathan could hear his leg moving up and down under the table. He was close to breaking.

"Do you have some sort of beef with the mayor?"

"No!"

"Frank," Ms. Thompson said. "Please don't say anything. Detective, I don't see why you're continuing the questioning. As I said, he's not going to answer. Besides, the charges are minor ones for which he'll likely get a slap on the wrist. I don't even know why we're sitting here."

"You're probably right. However, I think Frank is worried about something. Maybe even something that might implicate him in another crime, possibly one worse than disturbing the peace. If that's the case, it would certainly be to his advantage to come forward with that information voluntarily before we figure it out." He looked at Frank. "And, we will figure it out, at which time more charges will be filed and eventually a conviction made sending you up for a long time."

He could see Frank's expression start to change to panic.

"Could I speak to my client alone, please?" Ms. Thompson asked.

"I'll be right outside the door." Nathan stepped out into the hallway, almost walking into Detective Denzinger. "Sorry, Sam. I didn't expect anyone here."

"One of the officers told me you were down here."

"I'm questioning the guy who harassed the mayor's wife, but I think he's into something more."

"Most of them are." Denzinger said.

"Want to have some fun before you leave town?"

"You want to play a little good cop, bad cop in there?"

Nathan laughed. "Something like that."

The door opened and Ms. Thompson stuck her head out. "You can come back in."

Nathan went back into the room with Denzinger following him. "Frank, this is Detective Denzinger from the State Police Homicide Division.

"Homicide!" Frank looked at his lawyer.

"This is his attorney, Christina Thompson from Boston," Nathan told Denzinger.

"I know Ms. Thompson, by reputation only," Denzinger said.

Frank still starred at his attorney. "What's a homicide cop wanting from me?"

"Calm down. They're just trying to scare you," Ms.

Thompson said.

"Well, it's working."

Both Nathan and Denzinger did their best to hold back a laugh.

"That's enough! This questioning is over. Officer!" Ms. Thompson called to the correctional officer outside of the room. He opened the door and stepped in. "Please take my client back to his cell."

Frank and the correctional officer left the room.

She looked at Nathan. "I don't know what you think you're doing, but he's just a scared kid and if either of you talk to him like that again, I'll file a complaint." She picked up her leather bag and walked out of the room.

"I think we hit a nerve," Nathan said.

"That woman is a tough broad," Denzinger said. "She represents some of the top crooks in Boston. What's she doing here with that kid?"

"That's what I want to know. She said her firm does pro bono work sometimes."

"Believe me, the firm she works for never works for free. It doesn't make sense she's here."

"That's why I said I thought he was into something else."

"Send me his file. I'll check on some things in Boston and if I turn up anything, I'll get back to you," Denzinger said.

"I'd really appreciate that. Thanks." Nathan and Denzinger shook hands, and Denzinger left.

Nathan had an idea and wanted to check on something. He went to the booking area in the back corner of the building where he found Officer Barry Page at his desk. "Officer Page, I need to check on the booking of Frank Bishop."

Officer Page sat up at this desk. "What can I do for you?"

"Did Frank make a phone call after he was processed and if so, can I get the number he called?"

"He did make a phone call, but I don't have that information. You'll have to go see Mallory Duncan for the number." Page started typing on his computer. "He was booked in at eight-thirty and made his call twenty minutes later. Mallory will need that info to pull the number up."

"Thanks for your help."

Nathan walked to the front of the building where Mallory's office was. He found her on the phone when he got to her door and waited for her to finish.

She wrote something down, hung up her phone, and turned to him. "You need a number."

"You read my mind." He stepped in and sat in the chair next to her desk.

"That was Officer Page. He thought you might forget the info he gave you about Bishop's call, so he called me with it."

"So, he told you want I needed?"

"You need the number that Bishop called after he was booked."

"Yes."

Mallory started typing on her computer, inputting the information. It didn't take long for her printer to start. She pulled the page off of it and looked over it. "Here you go." She handed Nathan the paper.

It showed the time called, length of the call, and the number. "Perfect. Thank you. You're the best, Mallory."

She laughed. "I wish everyone agreed with you."

Nathan got up and went back to his office, taking a seat behind his desk. He picked up the phone and dialed the number.

"Please leave a message at the tone."

Nathan hung up the phone. That didn't help. At least for now.

He turned to his computer and pulled up a Probable Cause Affidavit to fill out for a warrant to search Frank Bishop's residence. After he finished typing, he attached it to an email and sent the request to the District Attorney. He then picked up the phone and dialed.

"District Attorney's Office, can I help you?"

"This is Detective Perry. I need to speak to Mr. Grant, if

possible."

"One moment, Detective." He was on hold.

In a short time, the DA picked up the call. "Nathan, I suppose you're calling about the request for a warrant I just received?"

"I am. What are my chances to get the judge to sign it?"

Grant paused. "You don't have anything that connects him to any of the Mano Island burglaries, do you?"

"Just a hunch."

"I'm not sure the judge will sign off on just a hunch."

"Daniel, you've got to try. I'm running out of ideas. This kid has some hot shot lawyer from Boston representing him. He's into something deeper than just harassing the mayor and his wife."

"Who's his lawyer?" Grant asked.

Nathan took her card out of his pocket. "Christine Thompson, from Dolan, Armstrong and Evans. Do you know her?"

"Not her, but I know her firm. They're one of the biggest criminal law firms in Boston. You many be right about him being involved in something else, but that still doesn't give enough probable cause for a warrant. I'll talk to the judge, but you need to try and come up with something else."

"Thanks, Daniel. I appreciate you doing what you can."

As soon as he hung up his phone, it rang again. "Detective Perry."

"Detective, this is Officer Wheeler at the front desk. Joe Cassidy is here to see you."

"What does he want?"

"I don't know, sir."

"He's standing right there, isn't he?"

"Yes, sir."

"Send him to my office." Nathan started clearing his desk. He didn't want Joe to see any new information on the burglaries."

Joe walked into the office. "Nathan, I hope I haven't

come at a bad time."

"There's never really a good time at the P.D. What can do for you today?" He motioned for him to sit down.

"I talked to Mr. Adams about his break-in. The last one that happened. He told me you suspected the thieves were after laptops to get into bank accounts."

Nathan let out a deep breath. "That's true."

"You didn't tell me about that break-in." He waved his finger at Nathan.

"It just slipped my mind."

"If I hadn't read about in the newspaper, I wouldn't have known. Anyway, I just spoke with Mr. Adams this morning and he said that bank told him an attempt had been made to get into his account, but they stopped it."

"I wasn't notified of that," Nathan said.

"I know. He just found out this morning and was going to call you, but I told him you and I were working on this case together and I would let you know."

"Joe, I need more information than just knowing there was an attempt." He stopped himself from saying more.

"I'd be glad to get whatever more you need," Joe anxiously offered.

"I appreciate it, but what I need can only be released to the police department. I'll take care of it." Nathan stood, hoping Joe would take the hint to leave. "Thanks for stopping by and letting me know."

Joe stood also. "I'm going to need a copy of the Adams' file."

"I'll have a copy made and delivered to your office tomorrow."

"I'd appreciate that. Thanks." He shook Nathan's hand and left.

Nathan sat back down and opened the folder from the Adams' burglary and dialed a number.

"Mystic State Bank. How can I help you?" the female voice said.

"This is Detective Nathan Perry from the Mystic Police Department. I need to speak to Mr. Kent."

"Let me see if he's available, detective." She put him on hold.

Midnight Confessions by the Grass Roots started playing on the line. At least the music is good, he thought to himself.

Before the song even got to the chorus, Bobby Kent came on the line. "Detective, what can I do for you?"

"I'm investigating the burglary at James Adams' home and understand that an attempt was made to hack into Mr. and Mrs. Adams' bank account. I wanted to see what information you had on that."

"Let me see. I think I have that information on my desk here somewhere. He told me you might be calling."

Nathan could hear papers being shuffled around.

"Yes, here it is. An attempt was made at two a.m. this morning. Because we had put additional security on his account, per Mr. Adams request, they didn't make it past the firewall."

"Why didn't you report that to this department?"

"I called Mr. Adams and he said he'd notify you."

Nathan looked at his ceiling and let out a deep breath. "I'm going to email you a list of account numbers that are connected to the burglaries on Mano Island. Would you please notify me if any of the accounts have been hacked or if an attempt is made to access them in some way other than by the customer?"

"I would need approval from the account owners first or a warrant."

"I'll get those approvals for you and have them delivered to your bank."

"Do you have my email address?" Kent asked.

"I have it from the bank's web site. In return, would you email me a copy of the report showing the attempt on Mr. Adams' account?"

"Yes, I'd be glad to."

"Thank you, Mr. Kent."

"You're most welcome, detective."

Nathan hung up his phone. He turned to his computer and typed up a release form for the burglary victims to sign allowing the bank to release information to the police department about their accounts. He then emailed the document to Gloria, asking her to have one of the clerks make copies and bring them to him. He looked at the wall clock and was glad to see his day was about over.

****

The following day, Gloria visited several antique shops in Boston looking for the stolen signs. So far, she'd had no luck after checking four stores.

Parking her car, Gloria started walking to the fifth one on her list. This store looked a little different than the others. It had a black magic look to it. The window had sculptures, pottery, bottles, and a morter and pestle.

She opened the door and stepped inside. The lighting in the shop was a bit darker than the previous stores she had been in, and the smell of incense nearly overpowered her.

She gazed at the walls, looking at the portraits of who she assumed were supposed to be witches. Then, she saw the first lead she'd had all day. On the wall, behind a counter in the back of the shop, was the sign from the Mystic newspaper office.

"Can I help you?" a male voice said from behind her. She nearly jumped out of her skin.

Gloria turned to find an older, white-haired gentleman dressed in a vintage black suit, complete with black cape. She found her breath and hoped her heart rate would slow soon. "Yes, I'm interested that sign up there with the witch on it." She looked around and didn't see any surveillance cameras.

The gentleman stepped past her and strolled to the

counter below the sign. Gloria followed. "You have an interest in the witchcraft?" he asked, his voice keeping in character of his costume.

"It's something that I recently developed. What is the price for the sign?"

"That particular item is five-hundred dollars."

She couldn't believe it. "Why so much?"

"It's a rare artifact that was discovered in a witch's home in Salem. We obtained it recently in an estate sale."

Gloria wanted to see how far the gentleman would go with his lies. "Can you provide a certificate of authenticity for it?"

"Of course, I can."

"You sure you don't want to rethink your answer. I'm Gloria Wheeler from the Mystic Police Department. I'm here investigating the theft of that sign as well as some others."

"Do you have some identification?" he asked.

Gloria placed her rather large purse on the counter and showed the shop owner her badge and I.D. "Where did you really get that sign?"

"A man brought it in to sell." His voice noticeably changed to a normal range, and he sounded somewhat shaken. "I swear I didn't know it was stolen. He brings in signs like that every couple weeks."

"You didn't bother asking him where he gets the signs?"

"I just assumed they were from estate sales. I never asked."

Gloria was skeptical. "Do you have his name and address?"

"Only a first name, Bill. But, I don't think it's his real name?"

"Why do you say that?" she asked.

"Because that's him on the front page of the newspaper in your bag and it doesn't say Bill."

Gloria pulled the paper out of her bag and looked at the photo. "Him? You're sure that's the man that sold you the sign?"

"He's sold me five of them. This one is the only one that hasn't been purchased."

"I need to see your identification and I'm going to need to take that sign with me. It's evidence."

"Am I under arrest?" He handed her his driver's license.

"No, but you are a witness. I'm going to call the Boston P.D. and have one of their officers take your official statement. I hope you have no travel plans for the near future." She pulled her cell phone out and made the call.

Later that night

Ricky walked into the warehouse where he and Frank usually met the boss. He was edgy about this meeting. His boss sounded angry on the phone when he called. He went to the back office where he found him waiting.

The boss paced while he talked. "Ricky, come in and sit down." He sat in the only other chair in the room. "Frank's been arrested."

"Arrested? What for?"

"Right now, just harassment, but we need to make sure he doesn't talk about anything else. I hired an attorney for him and she'll keep me updated on the case."

"He won't say anything," Ricky said. "He knows better than that."

"He better. It's both your and my heads on the block." He continued pacing. "What did you do with all the stuff you two stole?"

"We gave the laptops to you, and Frank and me split the other stuff between us. I fenced mine, but I don't know what Frank did with his."

"Well, that's just great. If the police get a warrant to search his place, we could be in big trouble."

"I'll go get Frank's stuff out of his place."

"Do you have a key?"

"No, but I can break in," Ricky said.

"If the police are watching his place, you'll get arrested too." He took a cell phone out of his pocket and dialed a number. "There's a problem," he said after someone answered. "Frank Bishop may have some of the stolen items at his home." The boss listened to the person on the other end of the call. "Thanks." He ended the call.

"What?" Ricky asked.

"The police brought a homicide detective in from the State Police to question him today. Are you two sure you haven't said anything to anyone?"

"Nothing, boss. Nothing. I swear."

"You stay away from Frank until his attorney gets him released and until things cool off a bit. No more burglaries, and when he does get released, stay away from him. Understand?"

"But we had another job planned for next week. Some old lady's house. It would be the easiest one yet."

"Not another break-in!" He grabbed Ricky by his shirt collar, pulling him to a standing position. "If either of you go against me, you'll will end up like Raymond Miller. Just remember that."

"I got it."

The man let go of his shirt, and Ricky didn't move one step until his boss left the warehouse. Then, he slumped back down into the chair.

Chapter Thirteen

Nathan spent most of Monday morning going over the burglary cases. He needed something to tie in Frank Bishop, but he wasn't having any luck. Spinning his chair around, he leaned back, staring out the window.

The sun was shining, and the snow had long melted away. It looked like a beautiful day outside, if it weren't for the twenty degree temperature. The newspaper on the credenza behind his desk caught his attention.

That made him think of Dana. He hadn't seen or heard from her in a few days. Maybe he should give her a call and see if she was available for lunch today.

He turned his chair back to his desk and found Gloria standing at his door.

"I'm sorry, I didn't want to disturb your thoughts," she said.

"I wasn't really in deep thought, just giving my eyes a break from reading these files. What can I do for you?"

Gloria came in and sat down in front of his desk. "I waited until my break time to come talk to you. I spent all day Saturday in Boston visiting antique stores looking for the stolen signs."

"I forgot you were going to do that. Did you have any luck?"

"Did I?" Her eyes widened. "I found the sign from the

newspaper office and the owner of the store was able to identify the person that sold him the sign."

"How did he identify him?"

She took the front page of Saturday's newspaper from the file folder and placed it in front of Nathan. "The store owner saw this in my bag."

Nathan picked up the newspaper and looked at the photo. "John Hawkins? Mystic's City Clerk is the sign thief? How sure is the owner about this? This photo isn't that good."

"I was as skeptical as you, but I showed him a photo of Hawkins from Mystic's official web site and he confirmed it. He's so sure that he gave a statement to a Boston PD officer." She handed Nathan the statement and he gave her back the newspaper. "He said Hawkins sold him five signs, but he only had this one left."

"What about some sort of identification when the store owner bought the sign?"

"He didn't get one and Hawkins demanded cash payment. There also were no cameras in the store, so we only have his signed statement. I have the sign from the newspaper office locked in my car and will need to log it in as evidence, if you wouldn't mind carrying it in for me."

Nathan read the store owner's statement again and smiled. "This is really big, Gloria. You did some great work."

She blushed. "Thank you. I'd love to go with you when you arrest him."

"I think we need to bring in him for questioning before we officially arrest him. We need to find out who the other person was at the newspaper office, but I don't see why you can't go when we bring him in for the questioning. Let me talk to the D.A. and I'll let you know what happens next."

Gloria got up to leave. "Don't forget we need to get the sign out of my car."

"I'll come get you as soon as I call Daniel Grant."

She started to walk out the door, but Nathan called her back. "Gloria. Good job."

She smiled from ear to ear and left.

Nathan picked up the phone and called Daniel Grant.

"District Attorney's office. Can I help you?" the secretary asked.

"This is Nathan Perry. Can I speak to Mr. Grant?"

"He's on another line right now, detective. I'm not sure how long he'll be. Do you want to wait or leave a message?"

"If you could have him call me as soon as he can at the police department."

"I'll tell him as soon as he's free."

"Thank you." Nathan hung up the phone. *Maybe today is going to be a good day after all.* A knock at the door interrupted his thoughts.

"Detective, do you have a minute?" It was Officer Avery.

"Sure, Ryan. Come in." The young officer came in and stood in front of the desk. "I have some of the signed release forms you needed from the Mano Island burglaries." He handed the forms to Nathan.

"Some of the forms?" Nathan looked through them.

"Yes. A few of the residents didn't want to sign, but said they would contact the bank themselves to see if their account was accessed."

"Are they going to tell us what they find out?"

"They said they would, but I have a feeling I'll have to follow up with them."

"You're probably right." Avery turned to leave. "Ryan, wait. Could you do me a favor?"

"Sure. What do you need?"

"I'm expecting a call from the D.A. and I don't want to miss it. Gloria has one of the stolen signs in her car that she recovered that she needs to have brought in and logged as evidence. Could you carry it in for her? She's working the front desk and will need to walk with you so as not to break the chain of evidence."

"I'd be glad to." He turned to leave.

"Thanks," Nathan called after him.

A few minutes later, his phone rang. "Detective Perry." He answered just as he saw Avery and Gloria walk past his office door on their way out to get the sign.

"Detective, this is Daniel Grant returning your call. I hope this isn't a bad time."

"Not at all. I have some news for you."

"I hope you have some evidence linking Frank Bishop to the burglaries because Judge Mason wouldn't sign the search warrant."

"Unfortunately, no. I don't have any new evidence yet."

"That's too bad. The judge said he needs more probable cause before he'll approve a search warrant."

"I'm still working on it. The news I do have has to do with the sign thefts. One of our officers located one of the signs in an antique store in Boston over the weekend and the store owner identified who sold him the sign."

"That's wonderful. Who was it?"

"You're not going to believe it. He identified John Hawkins as the person who sold not only that sign, but at least four others."

"Hawkins? You're right. I don't believe it," Grant said. "Who was the officer?"

"Gloria Wheeler was in the store and saw the sign. The owner saw Hawkins picture in a newspaper Gloria had. She then showed him Hawkins picture from the Mystic city web site and he confirmed it was him. Gloria even had a Boston P.D. officer take his sworn statement. I have it on my desk right now."

"She did a good job."

"That she did." Nathan looked up and saw Gloria walk back past his office with Avery carrying the sign behind her. "She's entering that sign into evidence right now."

"I'd say Officer Wheeler needs to go make an arrest," Grant said.

"I think you're right. I'll let you know when we have him in custody. I have a feeling he's not going to be too happy about it at all."

"Thanks, and let me know when you finally get something on Bishop."

"I will." Nathan hung up the phone and went to find Gloria.

Both Gloria and Officer Avery were standing at the evidence locker logging the sign in as evidence. "Gloria, I talked to the D.A. and he said to arrest Hawkins. Do you want to come with me and do the honors?"

"That's fantastic, Gloria," Avery said.

"I do, but I can't leave the front desk again."

"I want to fill the chief in on this before the arrest is made. I'll get it cleared by him," Nathan said. "Find someone to cover for you up there and I'll be right back."

Gloria had a frightful look on her face when Nathan headed to the chief's office. When he got there, he heard the chief on the phone and waited until he ended the call before he rounded the corner. Finally, he heard the chief hang up and he stepped into the doorway. "Chief, do you have a minute? I have some news."

"Perry, yes, come in. I hope its news about the murder. I talked to the mayor last night and he doesn't feel you've done enough to solve this case. I don't have to remind you that your job is on the line."

"You don't, but thanks for the reminder anyway." He stepped into the office and sat down. "We're about to make an arrest for the sign thefts in town."

"Really? Well, that is good news. Who is the suspect?" The chief picked up his coffee to take a drink.

"John Hawkins, the Town Clerk."

The chief started choking on his coffee. "John? I don't believe it. He's one of our most upstanding citizens."

"We have a confirmed identification of him as the person who sold five signs to an antique store in Boston."

"You spoke with this person who made the I.D.?" He wiped coffee from his face.

"No, sir. Officer Wheeler did the legwork on this over the weekend. She found the store and once the owner made the I.D., she called a Boston P.D. officer to take his sworn statement."

"Gloria did that? She doesn't work on weekends."

"She did this on her own time and is writing up the report right now. I'd like to go make the arrest and take Gloria with me. She did a fine job on this and the department should be proud of her." Nathan hoped he had backed the chief into a corner so he'd have to let Gloria make the arrest.

The chief paused before answering. "Well, I suppose she can go with you. As long as she isn't going to claim the weekend hours and she has to make sure the front desk is covered while gone."

"I'll see to it. Thank you."

"You're sure it was John Hawkins?"

"The storeowner confirmed it with his photo and I've already spoken with

Daniel Grant. He told me that's enough to make the arrest."

"I'll be interested to know why he did it."

"Yes, sir. We'll be speaking to him about that once we bring him in. Since it was the newspaper sign that was found, that also confirms that he was involved in the assault of the security guard too."

Chief Cabot shook his head in disgust. "Go arrest him."

Nathan hurried back down to the first floor, but made a stop at his office first. He picked up the phone and dialed.

"*Mystic Messenger*. How can I help you?"

"This is Detective Perry. I need to speak to Dana Tyler please."

"One moment." He was put on hold.

"This is Dana Tyler."

"Dana, its Nathan. You need to get a photographer down to City Hall right now."

"Why? What's going on?"

"We're about to arrest John Hawkins for the sign thefts and the assault on Ron Burns," he told her.

"John Hawkins! No."

"Gloria Wheeler and I are heading down there now. Can you be there?"

"You bet I can. Thanks." She hung up before he could even say goodbye.

Nathan walked up front and found Gloria at the front desk with Officer Cynthia Walker waiting to fill in. "Are you ready to go?"

"I am," Gloria said. "I'm a little nervous. I've never made an arrest before."

"You'll be fine." Nathan patted her on the shoulder.

"Go get 'em, Gloria. Make us proud," Officer Walker said.

City Hall was close enough to the police department that they could have walked, but they drove instead so they didn't parade a handcuffed Hawkins down the street. However, Nathan did park on the street in front, so they could walk him out the front door.

The two officers stopped at the door to the Town Clerk office before going in. Nathan wanted to make sure he was in there, and he wanted to make sure Gloria was ready. He also looked around, but didn't see Dana there yet. "Hawkins is in there. Are you ready for this?"

"I am."

"I want you to take the lead on this, but if you need me, I'll be right beside you," he assured her. He opened the door and Gloria stepped in first.

Hawkins looked up and smiled at the two officers, but before he could say a word, Gloria spoke. "John Hawkins, you're under arrest for theft and the assault of Ron Burns."

"What are you talking about? I haven't done anything," Hawkins said.

Gloria stepped around the counter and took out her handcuffs. Nathan followed her. She grasped Hawkins hand to put the handcuff on, but he tried to pull away. Gloria twisted his hand at his wrist and pushed him down onto the counter.

"Mr. Hawkins, I suggest you allow Officer Wheeler to do her job, or she may hurt you," Nathan said.

Hawkins stopped moving and Gloria finished handcuffing him. She pulled on the back of his shirt collar to help upright him.

"You're making a big mistake," he said.

"I don't think so," Nathan answered.

Gloria read him his rights as they walked around the counter to leave.

"At least take me out the back way," Hawkins pleaded.

"Sorry, I parked out front," Nathan said.

Word must have spread that Hawkins was being arrested because everyone had come out of their offices to watch him being taken out. He hung his head, not looking at anyone, as Nathan and Gloria walked him out. As soon as they walked outside, Dana and a photographer were there.

"Mr. Hawkins, why did you steal the signs and was it necessary to hurt Ron Burns the way you did?" Dana asked.

"I'm innocent. This is a big mistake. You'll see," he said.

Nathan looked at Dana, who mouthed, Thank you to him.

Back at the station, Hawkins was brought into the booking area. "Make sure you take full palm prints of both hands when you fingerprint him," Nathan told the booking officer. "Send them to Mallory for a comparison right away."

"Yes, sir," the officer answered.

Nathan and Gloria stepped aside to fill out the arrest form while Hawkins was being processed. "I want you to do the questioning of Hawkins," he told Gloria.

"Really? Are you sure?"

"Don't you think you can do it?"

"Of course, I can do it."

"Good. I'll be right there, if you need anything," he assured her.

"Detective, we're finished here," the booking officer

said.

"Thanks. Come on, Hawkins. It's time to talk." He handcuffed Hawkins again and led him out of the room with Gloria following.

They stepped into the interrogation room. Nathan sat Hawkins down on one side of the table, and Gloria sat down on the other side.

"Mr. Hawkins, you were read your rights, do you want an attorney present?" Nathan asked.

"I am an attorney, you idiot."

"There's no need for that tone. So, you do not want an attorney?"

"No, I do not."

"Very well." Nathan moved to the side of the room and leaned against the wall. He nodded to Gloria.

She opened the file folder she brought and began questioning. "Mr. Hawkins, you've been arrested for stealing the sign from the newspaper office and also for assault on Ron Burns, their security officer. We've recovered the stolen sign and a positive I.D. has been made that you were the one that sold the sign to the shop in Boston. Would you like to make a statement about that?"

"I did not steal the sign, nor hurt that security officer."

"The storeowner in Boston also said you sold him several other signs that we believe were stolen from Mystic businesses. We're in the process of recovering those signs from the people that purchased them."

"I didn't steal any signs. This is ridiculous. I'm an upstanding member of this community. Why would I do something like that?"

"That's what we're trying to find out, sir," Gloria said.

They heard a knock on the door and Mallory stepped in and handed Nathan a sheet of paper. He looked at it. "Thanks, Mallory." She left.

"Mr. Hawkins, your handprint has been matched to the handprint taken from the wall of the newspaper office after the theft," Nathan said, handing the paper to Gloria.

"I walk by that office all the time. I'm sure I've touched that wall many times."

Gloria looked at Nathan. He was sure she was stumped as to what to ask next.

"The handprint we recovered at the scene was at the exact location that the person who took the sign touched the wall. We have that on surveillance video. There won't be any disputing it once a jury sees that video," Nathan said.

Hawkins remained silent.

Gloria looked at Hawkins. "You had an accomplice at the newspaper office when you took the sign. Who was it?"

"I'm finished answering questions," Hawkins said.

"John," Nathan said, leaning over the table. "You know this will go much easier on you, if you cooperate. Now that we know you took the sign, it's only a matter of time before we find out who helped you and I guarantee, he will will sing like a bird when he's brought in."

"Don't forget that we'll get Ron Burns to identify you too," Gloria added.

"That's right. That would seal the deal. You're going to do a long sentence for this, John," Nathan said.

"Nonsense, for burglary?"

"Burglaries, plural, plus assault," Gloria reminded him.

Hawkins shifted in his chair. "I think I better have an attorney now."

"I think that's a wise decision." Nathan nodded for Gloria to follow him out of the room. In the hallway, they found Daniel Grant coming out of the observation room.

"That was good interrogation, Officer Wheeler," Grant told her.

"Thank you."

"Do we have enough for a conviction?" Nathan asked.

"If the evidence is as good as you said in there, I think we do. Get everything to my office and I'll get the charges filed. Good work, officers." Grant left.

The news of John Hawkins arrest was the talk of the town. Dana's story was front page news. All eyes were on Nathan when he walked into Ginger's the next morning. He took a seat in the booth close to the kitchen.

Ginger brought a cup over to his table and poured the coffee. "Is it true?"

"You don't waste small talk do you?"

"There's no time in my business. Everyone wants to know if its true. Well?"

He took a drink of coffee to prolong his answer. She stood waiting and he chuckled. "It's true."

"Wow." She said down across from him. "Tell me all about it."

"All I can say is that we are in the process of filing the charges, but he is in jail. Now, how about some breakfast?"

"You take all the fun out of being nosey." She laughed. "What can I get you?"

"I'd like to have two biscuits with gravy and a side of bacon."

"Coming right up." She got up and went to the kitchen.

Nathan took another drink of coffee and then saw Dana come into the cafe. When she spotted him, she came right to the table and sat down.

"Thanks for the scoop yesterday. Is there anything new?"

"Good morning to you," Nathan said.

"I'm sorry. Good morning."

Ginger came over and poured Dana some coffee. "Good story this morning."

"Thanks," Dana said.

"This is best news this town has had in a while," Ginger said.

"It'll be even better once we catch who killed Raymond Miller," Dana added. "I don't suppose you're close to making an arrest?" Dana asked.

"No comment," Nathan replied. Dana looked disappointed.

"What can I get you for breakfast, Dana?"

"I'll take a veggie omelet. Thanks."

Ginger went to the kitchen and Dana looked at Nathan. "Seriously, what can you tell me?"

"Officially, I can't tell you anything. You know that."

"Has Hawkins told who his accomplice was yet?"

"He's not saying much of anything since he asked for an attorney. We're still working on the accomplice, but hope to have that person in custody soon." Nathan took a drink of his coffee. "Make sure in your next article that the main credit goes to Gloria Wheeler. She did a lot of the leg work on this. She did a great job."

"I'll call her later for a quote."

"She tracked down the sign at an antique store in Boston. From there, she got the identification of the seller of the sign."

Dana started writing again, then looked up at Nathan. "And, that was Hawkins?"

"Yes."

"What about the other signs? Did he steal them also?"

"We believe he did, but have no evidence of that yet. We're still investigating."

Dana finished writing and put her pencil down. "Ron and his wife will be so glad to hear that an arrest has been made."

"I plan on calling him when I get back to the office."

Dana put her notepad away and took a sip of coffee. "Off the record now, when do you think you'll make the second arrest?"

"We really don't know. Hawkins wanted to represent himself until he realized how much we really knew. That's when he asked for an attorney. I'm not sure he'll tell us who the other person was."

"That's too bad."

"I have an idea. When will the next story about Hawkins' arrest come out in the newspaper?" Nathan asked.

"It will be in tomorrow's issue and probably the lead story on the front page again since we didn't have a lot of information for today's story."

"What if the story said we knew who the second person is and we're in the process of getting a warrant for his arrest? Add something about how it would go easier on the person, if they just turned themselves in."

"Maybe they would believe it and come in on their own," Dana added. She took her notepad out of her bag and started writing.

"Here you go," Ginger said, placing their breakfast on the table. "It looks like you two are up to something."

"No, Dana's just interviewing me about Hawkins arrest for her next article." Nathan took his fork and dug into the biscuits and gravy.

"Well, shoot, and I missed it. Do either of you need more coffee?"

"None for me, right now," Dana said.

Nathan couldn't speak with a mouthful of food, but shook his head no.

Ginger walked away as Dana showed Nathan what she had written. "How's this sound?"

He swallowed and read her notes. "Could you add something that whichever one of them gives us the details of the thefts first could get a lighter sentence?"

"Yes." She took her notepad back and scribbled that down.

"Now, we wait until tomorrow and see what happens," Nathan said, taking another bite of food.

After he and Dana finished their breakfast, Nathan headed to the police department. He was late getting in, and the morning briefing had just ended. The officers were coming out of the room, and as she came out, Gloria saw him coming down the hall.

She followed him into his office. "I wish you'd been at briefing this morning. They commended us on Hawkins' arrest. The chief even said I did a good job." She was all smiles.

"I wish I'd been there. You deserve all the accolades for

this. I think Dana Tyler may be calling you today for a quote from you for the newspaper article."

"Really? That's so exciting." She started to walk out, but stopped. "Oh, I almost forgot. Remember Mrs. Carson that lives on Mano Island?"

"The little blue-haired lady that I saw you talking to at the front counter one day?"

"Yes. Her son finally called me back about me looking at her security video. He's going to bring it in tomorrow. The chief said I could meet with Mr. Carson around ten in the morning. I was hoping you could meet with us when he gets here."

"I suppose I could do that. You asked the chief? That was brave of you."

"How could he tell me no after he had just commended me on my work?" She winked. "See you at ten." She walked out of his office.

Nathan went through the phone messages on his desk and found one from Joe Cassidy saying he needed to talk to him right away. He put that message in the 'to do later' pile and proceeded to sort through the other messages, before starting to return the calls.

After an hour of phone calls and answering emails, the final message left on his desk was Cassidy's. He decided to bite the bullet and call him.

"Hello, Cassidy Investigations."

"Joe, hello. It's Nathan Perry. I'm returning your call. What can I do for you?"

"Nathan, I just heard that you arrested John Hawkins."

"That's right, we did."

"I can't believe he would do anything like that. He's my accountant and lawyer, as well as my good friend. Is there anything I can do for him?"

He sounded honestly worried about his friend. "Joe, you might think about distancing yourself from him as quickly as possible. I don't think he's the person you think he is. You also might want to check your accounts to make sure he wasn't taking any money from you."

"He wouldn't steal from me. Can I come see him?" Cassidy asked.

"I don't think that would be a good idea. I'm sure his attorney will tell him not to speak to anyone."

"I just don't know what to do."

"Keep yourself busy on other things to keep your mind off of him." As soon as Nathan said it, he wished he hadn't.

"Good idea. Do you have anything new on the murder?"

"Nothing new yet, but I'll let you know when I do. If there's nothing else, I need to get back to work now," Nathan said.

"Sure. Thanks for calling, Nathan." Joe hung up, and Nathan did the same.

The next morning, Gloria walked into Nathan's office with a guest. "Detective, this is Dennis Carson. He brought the video in from his mother's surveillance system at her home."

Nathan stood and shook hands with Mr. Carson. "Thank you for coming in."

"I hope this helps you." He handed Nathan a computer disc.

"Our I.T. tech has set up a computer to a TV monitor in another room for us. Let's go there to view the video," Gloria said.

Mallory was waiting for them in the conference room when they walked in. Gloria handed the disc to Mallory and she, Nathan, and Mr. Carson sat in front of the TV monitor to view the video.

"I burned the disc with the last two weeks of surveillance," Mr. Carson said.

"Where do you want to start?" Mallory asked.

"Might as well start at the beginning, but real time will take too long, so can you speed it up? We'll just watch for anything unusual," Nathan said.

She started the video at three-times normal speed.

"How far back does your system keep the video before it loops over it?" Nathan asked.

"The system I set up for my mother will save about thirty days of video before looping," Carson said.

"Thirty days?" Mallory questioned.

Carson turned around. "I'm a computer programmer and wanted the best system I could find for my mother's home. I have cameras viewing each side of the house and will follow movement, if any." He turned to Nathan. "I live in Boston and don't get down here to see her as often as I'd like. I have the system set up so I can look at the video from my home also. Unfortunately, I just got home from an extended vacation and haven't checked it for a while. Officer Wheeler called and I burned the disc without looking at it yet."

"Your mother has been in a few times complaining about teenagers being around her house," Gloria said.

"She told me. Before my trip, I kept an eye out, but never saw anything."

"There's some movement there," Mallory said, slowing down the video.

On the monitor, they saw two men walking around the house checking windows.

"Those aren't teenagers," Carson said.

"No, but the one in front is Frank Bishop," Nathan said. "We have him in our jail on another charge right now."

"That's good to know, but what about the other guy?" Carson asked.

"I don't know who he is. Gloria?"

"I've never seen him before either."

"Mallory, can you get me a print of this and also a close-up of the other guy?" Nathan asked

"Yes, but the close-up will be blurry."

"That's okay. Can you also finish watching the video and see if anything else pertinent shows up?"

"I will."

"Mr. Carson, thank you for bringing the video in. I think

it will be a great help to us," Nathan said.

"I'm glad I could help."

"Are you going to tell your mother about this?" Gloria asked.

"I'm not sure. If you've talked to my mother, you know she gets confused easily. I will tell you that she'll be coming with me back to Boston. After seeing this, I'm not letting her stay in her home alone."

"We'll make sure a patrol car drives by her home," Nathan said.

"Thank you. If you're finished with me, I want to check on her and get her packed."

Nathan shook hands again and Gloria showed him how to get back to the front entrance. She came back in as Mallory was handing Nathan the photos she had just printed.

"What are you going to do now?" Gloria asked.

He held up the photos. "This should be enough to get our search warrant for Bishop's home. I'm going to call Daniel Grant to see about the warrant and then talk to Bishop to see if he'll tell me who that other guy is." Mallroy brought Nathan a second set of photos. He handed those photos to Gloria. "Will you take these to Sergeant Donnelly and ask him to show them at tomorrow morning's briefing and for a patrol car to check Mrs. Carson's house routinely until we identify the other guy?"

"I will" Gloria said.

Chapter Fourteen

After calling the District Attorney about the warrant, Nathan entered the interrogation room where Bishop was waiting. "Frank, I just have a few questions for you."

"Shouldn't my attorney be here?"

"I'm kind of in a rush, but after you hear the questions, if you still want her here I'll call her." He placed the surveillance photos in front of him. "Look familiar?"

Frank's eyes widened, but he didn't answer.

"Whose the other guy?"

"I can't answer."

"You know we'll figure it out, but it'll go so much better for you if you tell me now."

Frank stared at the photos. "I can't."

"You mean you won't." Nathan gathered the photos and put them back in the folder and stood. "I'll call your attorney."

"No!"

That response surprised Nathan and he sat back down. "You don't want me call your attorney?"

"If I tell you who the other guy is, I'll be killed."

"What does that have to do with your attorney?"

"My attorney works for my boss," Frank admitted. "Anything I say in front of her will be go right back to him."

"We can protect you."

"Not from this guy. I won't answer any of your questions.

Can I go back to my cell now?"

Nathan had the officer take Bishop to his cell. Back in his office, he called Sam Denzinger. "Sam, Nathan Perry. I hope I didn't catch you at a bad time."

"Not at all. What can I do for you?"

"Remember the interrogation you were in with me?"

"I do."

"Well, we got him and another guy on some surveillance video casing a house and when I questioned him about it, he admitted his lawyer works for his boss and if he talks, his life will be in danger. I was wondering if you could find out who that lawyer's main client is."

"What was her name again?"

"Christine Thompson, of Dolan, Armstrong and Evans."

"Right. I was going to check around on her and forgot. Let me do that and I'll get right back to you."

"Thanks, I'd really appreciate it." Just as Nathan hung up the phone, Hank walked in.

"I brought you something." Hank handed him the search warrant he'd requested.

"Thanks. I could use some help with this search. Want to come?"

"I sure do."

"One thing first." He picked up the phone and punched in a number. "Mallory, I have a search warrant for Frank Bishop's home and I'd like for you to go with Hank and I to log any evidence we find. I want to go right now. Can you come with us?"

"Just let me get my case and I'll be right there."

It only took a few minutes for Mallory to get to Nathan's office and the threesome left to do their search. Nathan and Hank drove in a patrol car and Mallory took the department's van to carry any evidence they might find.

Upon arriving at the house, the two officers stepped on the porch first. Nathan turned to Mallory. "Wait out here until we clear the house."

"Did you contact Bishop's lawyer about the search?" Hank asked.

"I forgot." He smiled. "I guess I'll have to call her after we get back to the office."

The door was locked, but it didn't take much of a push for Nathan to open it. He and Hank checked each room and closet before they declared it clear. Back on the porch, they all put on rubber gloves to preserve any fingerprints the evidence might have.

They searched the living room first. Finding nothing, Mallory set up in there to collect and log anything else they found. In the bedroom closet of the small home, they found a box that contained jewelry, a police scanner, three cameras, and two handguns. They brought those items out for Mallory to photograph and log.

"There's an old building out back. I'm going to go look out there. Hank, stay here with Mallory."

That building was not locked, and inside Nathan found a boat motor, likely belonging to Mr. Wright. He also found life jackets, a marine radio, and cans of fuel. Nathan went back inside the house.

"I found the items from Mr. Wright's boathouse in the shed. Let's get all of this loaded in the van. Did you find any computers?"

"No, none at all," Mallory said.

After the evidence was loaded into Mallory's van, they all headed back to the police department.

"This is going to take forever to get everything logged and results back. I'm going to need help with this." Mallory told Nathan as she got out of the van.

"Check with Sergeant Donnelly to see if he can loan a couple of patrol officers to help," Nathan said.

Mallory rolled her eyes. "You know that patrol officers don't think it's their job to do something like that."

"Don't we have some rookie officers?"

"We do. You're one of them," she teased.

Nathan laughed at her joke. "I'll talk to Donnelly and see what I can do about getting you some help without them complaining."

"Thank you."

They moved all of the evidence into one of the large meeting rooms, and after everything was in, Mallory locked the door and placed a piece of tape labeled evidence across the door, taking the key with her to preserve the chain of evidence.

Nathan went to his office and walked in just as his phone was ringing. "Detective Perry." He sat down behind his desk.

"Nathan, this is Sam Denzinger. I wanted to get back to you as soon as I found out the information you needed about Bishop's attorney."

"You work fast. What did you find out?"

"Her firm does represent several known white-collar criminals, but none of them really jump out as the type that would hire a two-bit thug like Bishop to do those burglaries."

"Damn, I was really hoping something would stand out. What about anyone with lesser crimes than white-collar?"

"Nothing. The guys I talked to here said no one other than corporations and their executives could afford them."

"What corporations does Miss Thompson work with?" Nathan could hear Denzinger thumbing through pages of papers.

"Boston Beverage, the Revere Insurance Agency, the Hale Clothing company, First Bank of Boston, Parker Pharmaceutical, and Boston General Hospital."

"Those are all reputable companies. Anything else?"

"That's all I have for now about that. I'll email you the list and if I find out anything else, I'll let you know. I do have another piece of information you may be interested in."

"What's that?"

"Our Cyber Crime unit traced the money that was taken from the accounts. I'm emailing their report to you now. I think you'll find where the money ended up interesting."

"Thanks, Sam." Nathan hung up the phone. He leaned back in his chair. An email dinged and he saw it was the list from Denzinger.

Opening the email, he stared at the list. Something about this list was familiar to him, but he couldn't place what it was. The second email was even more interesting than Denzinger said. He hit print and then placed the document in a file folder.

Wednesday night

Ricky Carter knew this would be a more difficult break-in without Frank to help him, but he was sure he could do it. He'd show the boss that he was perfectly capable of handling jobs on his own. He checked his watch that showed a little after one a.m. Time to go. He got into his car and drove to Mano Island.

Ricky parked in the usual hiding spot that he and Frank always used when they did the other jobs on the island. The neighborhood was quiet and the sky cloudy, perfect weather for the job at hand. He made his way through the trees behind the houses, continuing to the house that was the target for the night, Mrs. Carson's.

He had been studying the house for quite a while and knew there was a blind spot at the rear corner of the house that the motion detector lights didn't cover. He slowly crept up in that area until he reached the rear window.

Using the crowbar he carried to force the window open, he climbed in. He pulled a large cloth bag out of the backpack he wore and began putting things inside. Ricky had seen the old lady leave with some guy, so he wasn't worrying about noise. He bumped into a table and knocked a lamp to the floor breaking it. "Damn it."

Ricky then started to the rear of the house where the bedroom was to see what kind of jewelry the old lady had. Just as he reached the door, the light came on and he looked up to find himself face to face with Mrs. Carson, who had a handgun pointed right at him.

"What are you doing in my house?" she shrieked.

He saw her hand was shaking and pulled his own gun. "Lady, put your gun down. I'm pretty sure I'm a better shot than you and this will not end well, if I shoot."

He could see she was scared, and the gun shook even more as he inched closer until he finally grabbed it from her hand. "You aren't supposed to be here. I saw a guy load you and some suitcases in his car and drive off."

"That was my son and I came home."

"Get back into your room and sit on the bed," Ricky ordered. He took the cloth belt from her robe and tied her hands in front of her.

"Not too tight please," she begged.

"Where's your jewelry?"

"I don't have anything of value," she said, her voice whimpering.

Before he could ask again, he heard a siren. He motioned for her to get up and gently pushed her into the living room.

****

Nathan's cell phone rang, waking him up from a sound sleep. "Hello," he mumbled.

"Detective Perry, it's Mary from the police department. Detective, are you awake?"

"I'm awake. What's going on?" He sat up on the side of the bed.

"There was a break-in on Mano Island and the homeowner is being held hostage."

That news woke Nathan right up and he grabbed his pants. "Whose home?"

"Caroline Carson. She's an elderly resident."

"I'm familiar with her. Call Officer Gloria Wheeler, fill her in, and tell her to meet me there. I'm on the way."

Nathan arrived at the scene twenty minutes later. Among the three police cars there, he saw Ryan Avery standing behind a police car and walked up to him. "What's the update, Ryan?"

"He entered through a back window. His said his name is Ricky and he has Mrs. Carson in there with him. That's all we know for now. He's not talking much."

Gloria arrived and rushed up to them with another man. "What's happening?"

"I thought Mrs. Carson was at her son's house," Nathan said. He looked past Gloria at the man standing behind her.

"This is my husband, Steve," she said.

"Nice to meet you, detective, even under these circumstances."

Nathan nodded to him as they shook hands. He looked back at Gloria. "Mrs. Carson is a hostage."

"Dispatch told me. I called her son while we drove here. He said she wouldn't stay with him and he had to bring her home. He was planning on coming down in the morning and trying to convince her again. He's on his way from Boston now."

"Ryan, how did we know about the break-in?" Nathan asked.

"The alarm company called," Avery replied.

"Is he armed?"

"He said he was, but no shots have been fired."

"Hand me your car microphone and make sure it's on speaker." Nathan noticed several neighbors were now gathering on the street. "Contact the PD and get some more officers out here for crowd control. We need everyone off this street and it blocked off."

"Yes, sir." Avery reached into the car and handed Nathan the microphone and then stepped away to request more officers to move the bystanders away.

"Ricky, this is Detective Perry. I'd like to come in and talk to you," he said over the speaker.

No response.

"Come on, Ricky. We don't want this to end badly. Let me come in and talk about it."

The front door finally opened, and Mrs. Carson stood there with Ricky behind her. "He said you can come in, but only if you don't have a gun," she shouted as best as she could.

Nathan removed his gun from his back waistband and handed it to Gloria.

"You're not really going in there unarmed, are you?" Gloria asked.

"I've got a small gun on my ankle. If I can get him to release Mrs. Carson, you need to get her from the house to safety."

Gloria nodded.

He walked to the house and stepped inside. Ricky still had Mrs. Carson before him, in the doorway to the kitchen. Nathan held his hands in the air in front of him.

"Close the door behind you and lock it," Ricky ordered. "Turn around so I can see that you don't have a gun.

Nathan did that. "Are you okay, ma'am?"

"Yes."

"Ricky, why don't you let her go. I'll stay and we'll figure this out."

His eyes darted from Nathan to the windows and back to Nathan.

"You don't want to hurt her, Ricky. If that happens, I can guarantee that every officer outside will come rushing in here and you'll be carried out in a body bag."

Ricky thought for a few seconds. "Okay, she can go, but you move away from the door."

"Ma'am, there will be a police woman outside that will come up to help you away from the house." Nathan stepped to the side of the room and Ricky released Mrs. Carson.

She slowly walked to the door and outside. Nathan could see Gloria rush up and hold onto Mrs. Carson as she helped her to the ambulance that had just arrived.

"Thank you, Ricky. That shows good faith on your part. I'm Nathan, let's sit down and talk about what's going to happen."

"No. We'll stand right here. If I hear anyone come into the house, you're a dead man."

"If that happens, you'll be a dead man too. Let's face it, you aren't going to leave this house alive unless you're in handcuffs."

"It wasn't supposed to happen this way," Ricky said. "She wasn't supposed to be home. I was going to show my boss that I could do this all by myself."

"Your boss? Is that Frank Bishop?"

"No, Frank's my partner. He never thought I could do anything myself either, but I showed him when I saved us from the guy that came in through the garage. I took care of him."

"You're talking about Raymond Miller. You did show him, all right," Nathan said, playing along.

"Damn right."

"Your boss didn't like what you did to Mr. Miller, did he?"

"Neither him or Frank liked it, but look at me now. I got a police officer as my hostage."

"What's your boss' name?"

Ricky waved his gun at Nathan. "I'm not falling for that. I need to think."

"All I need is his name and it will go a lot better for you," Nathan said.

"Shut up!"

He noticed Ricky was shaking, and he looked like he was losing control. There was no way Nathan could get to his ankle gun while standing there, without Ricky firing at him first.

"Look Ricky, let's get real about this. The police will not negotiate for my release. If you can give me information on your boss, I promise to talk to the District Attorney to get lesser charges filed on you. If you don't help me, it's going to be a murder charge for Miller and depending on how I end up, it could be a murder of a police officer charge added on and you won't see the outside of a prison for the rest of your life. That's assuming that you get out of this situation alive."

Ten minutes later, Nathan opened the front door of the house and walked a handcuffed Ricky Carter out to Officer Avery, who put him into his police car. Avery handed Nathan back his firearm.

"Take him in and file charges for hostage taking, and along with burglary, charge him with Raymond Miller's murder." By this time, the sun was rising and Hank had arrived at the scene. Nathan looked at Hank and quietly said, "We have a big problem. Can you follow me to the District Attorney's office? I don't want to discuss it here or at the PD."

Nathan had called ahead to make sure Daniel Grant was in his office when he and Hank arrived. The secretary waved them ahead in, and Grant was waiting for them in his office.

"Gentlemen, this must be important to meet with me so early in the morning," Grant said. "Can I get you a cup of coffee?

"I could sure use one," Nathan said. Hank agreed.

Grant poured them each a cup from the coffee maker behind his desk and handed the cups to the men. "Let's hear what you have."

"We arrested Ricky Carter this morning when he broke into another house on Mano Island and held Caroline Carson hostage," Nathan said.

"I saw all the police cars when I left the house this morning. There must be more to it than burglary and hostage-taking."

"There is. He confessed to me that he killed Raymond Miller when he and Frank Bishop broke into the Miller's home."

Grant smacked his hands together. "Excellent. You caught the guy."

"We did, but that's not the most important part."

Grant looked confused. "What's more important than

catching a murderer?"

Nathan looked at Hank, who also looked confused, and then back to Grant. "It's who Ricky said their boss is."

"Who is it?" Grant asked.

Nathan let out a deep breath. "He said Mayor Newcomb hired he and Frank to burglarize all the homes."

Grant sat up straight in his chair. "Our Mayor Newcomb? Are you sure?"

"It all makes sense. Bishop went to see the mayor at his home and at his office and when he couldn't find him there, he went ballistic. Bishop also told me he couldn't talk in front of his attorney because everything would go straight back to his boss. I found out from the State Police that one of her clients is Boston General Hospital and more importantly, they tracked the money taken from the hacked accounts to a bank account linked to Newcomb."

"Boston General is where Newcomb was the Chief Financial Officer before he was elected mayor here," Hank said.

"Exactly. I would think that was a pretty big cut in pay for him to go from CFO to a mayor of a small town. The State Police emailed me the information about the accounts yesterday."

"You weren't kidding about it being big," Grant said.

"Dan, I'd like to keep this as quiet as possible, including keeping it from Chief Cabot," Nathan requested.

"The chief works at the pleasure of the mayor. I don't want to take a chance on him not believing the information and tipping the mayor off."

"I understand. Let me get that warrant for Newcomb's bank accounts. I'm pretty sure the judge will sign off on that today. If the bank information pans out and with Ricky Carter's statement and the information you gathered from the State Police, I can get you a warrant for his arrest," Grant said.

"The quicker the better," Nathan added.

I'll try to get it to you by the end of the day."

"Thank you." Nathan and Hank got up and left.

Outside of the courthouse, the two officers stopped to talk. "Remember, this is need to know only and no one but us needs to know," Nathan said.

"Just call me when you're ready to make the arrest. I want to be there," Hank said.

"You know I will." Nathan got in his car, and Hank headed out on patrol.

Nathan walked into the police department and stopped at his office to remove his jacket first. He then headed to the break room for more coffee, and hoped that someone picked up some donuts this morning. He missed breakfast and was hungry. After pouring his coffee and picking up a couple donuts, he went back to his office.

Gloria followed him inside and sat down. "Here's Officer Avery's report from this morning. All it needs is what happened with you and Ricky inside the house."

"Thanks. How is Mrs. Carson?" He took a bite of donut.

"I went with her in the ambulance and took her to the hospital where she was checked out. Other than her blood pressure being a little high, she's fine. Her son took her back to his home in Boston. I think if he has to handcuff her to a chair to keep her there, he will. He had no idea that she had a gun in her home."

"I'm glad to hear she's doing well."

"What the hell is going on with you? You are definitely not yourself this morning," Gloria said.

Nathan laughed a little at her language. "I'm fine. I didn't get much sleep last night and did spent some time with Ricky Carter holding a gun on me this morning. A couple cups of coffee and I'll be fine."

"You're right. I'm sorry. I'm on a third cup already myself. Call me, if you need anything." Gloria left the office.

Nathan got up and closed his office door. He sat back down and called Sam Denzinger, to tell him the news and ask if he wanted to be there for the arrest.

"I think I better sit this one out. You deserve all the accolades, not the State Police. This was your case," Denzinger said. "I'll stop by in a few days to see you."

"Thanks, Sam. I'll see you then." As soon as he hung up the phone, it rang. "Detective Perry."

"Perry, why haven't you filled me in on what happened last night on Mano Island. Get your ass up to my office now!" Chief Cabot ordered.

"Yes, sir." Nathan wasn't looking forward to this conversation and he really hoped that the mayor was not there. He headed upstairs to the chief's office and was relieved to find him alone.

"Perry, come in and sit down," Chief Cabot said. "I've read Officer Avery's report, but your part of the report was not included. You want to fill me in on what happened inside that house?"

"I just got to my office about an hour ago and it's been nonstop work since I arrived. I really haven't had time to write up my report yet. I'll get it to you as soon as I can."

"What charges are you planning on filing on---" he put his glasses on and looked at his computer screen, "Ricky Carter?"

"Well, sir, there will be a breaking and entering charge from last night and, of course, hostage-taking. While speaking to Mr. Carter inside the house, he did indicate that he was responsible for Raymond Miller's murder."

"Excellent."

"However, he had not been read his rights yet and he'll have to be questioned again. I'm sure he'll ask for an attorney to be present and I doubt very much if his attorney will allow him to confess to murder again. Regardless, I spoke with the District Attorney this morning and we're working on getting those charges filed somehow."

"Good work. I'll phone the mayor about this. I'm sure he'll be pleased with your progress."

"Sir, if you wouldn't mind waiting a while before

informing the mayor about this. I think it will work better for all involved," Nathan suggested.

"Why would I want to wait? This is the best news this department has had in months."

"The mayor is a politician, and as such, he will want to make a statement to the press. That could tip off Bishop and Carter's boss. They both have alluded to having a boss, but not said too much about him. I think we can persuade them to name that person. If the press gets wind of Carter's arrest, I think this so-called boss will be in the wind and we'll never get him."

Chief Cabot didn't say anything for several seconds. "I suppose you're right, but I don't like keeping things from the mayor."

"I'm sure it won't be long before we come up with something and an announcement can be made."

"I suppose so, but you let me know as soon as you come up with something," the chief said.

"Will do." Nathan got up and left before the chief changed his mind.

It took Nathan the rest of the morning to type up his part of the report of the previous night's events. He was careful not to include anything about the mayor. After he hit save on the computer, he sat back in his chair and typed up the real report, including the mayor's name.

He let out a deep breath. This had been a difficult investigation and one that had his career on the line. Hopefully, in the end, the chief would make him a permanent member of the Mystic Police Department.

Nathan's stomach started growling. *Donuts aren't the most filling breakfast,* he thought and decided to walk to Ginger's for lunch. He let Gloria know where he was going when he passed the front counter.

For February, it was an unusually warm day with the temperature in the mid-fifties. It was great weather for walking to lunch. He reached Ginger's and went inside. Now that he had been back in Mystic for a while, he recognized many of the usual lunchtime crowd at the café and nodded or said hello to them. He took a seat in a booth near the counter and grabbed a menu from the table.

It didn't take long for Ginger to approach. "Coffee today?"

"No, I think I'll have a Coke today."

"Do you know what you want to eat, or do you need a little more time?"

"What's your special today?"

"My famous Chicken Pot Pie."

"I'm pretty hungry today and that sounds perfect."

"Coming right up. I heard there was some kind of ruckus on Mano Island last night," Ginger said.

"There was, but nothing I can talk about right now."

"You keep thinking that. Dana is heading your way."

"Hi, Ginger. Can I have some hot tea and a chicken salad wrap, please?" Dana asked, sliding into the booth across from Nathan.

"Absolutely." Ginger headed to the kitchen.

"By all means, please sit down," Nathan said, jokingly.

"Oh, did you not want me to sit here?" Dana asked.

"I'm just kidding. Yes, you can sit there."

She removed her coat, placed it next to her, and then pulled a small notepad and pen from her purse. "I called and left you a couple messages this morning. Didn't you get them?"

"I've been working since about two a.m. and haven't had a chance to check my messages. This is my first break."

"That's what I wanted to talk to you about. What can you tell me about what happened last night?" she asked.

Nathan knew he shouldn't be surprised by her question. After all, that was her job just as much as last night was his. "We're still investigating."

"Oh, come on. You have to have more than that."

"Dana, I'm working on about four hours of sleep. Chances

are that I wouldn't even give you the right information. We'll have a press release ready probably by three o'clock."

"Can you at least confirm that it was Caroline Carson's home that the police were at last night?"

He gave in. "Okay, here's all I can give you. Mrs. Carson's home was broken into last night and her alarm system notified the police. She was taken hostage and released soon as the police arrived at her house. She was taken to the hospital where she was later released to her son. From what I understand, she's doing well. The burglar was arrested."

"Was the person who broke in to her home the same as the other break-ins on the island and who was arrested?" she asked.

"I told you that's all I can say."

Ginger came back to their table with the drinks and food. "Did he tell you anything?" she asked Dana.

"Not really. He did say that Caroline Carson was taken hostage last night, but released."

"Is she okay?' Ginger asked Nathan.

"She's fine. No more questions about last night, okay?"

"Okay, but you will call me first with anything new, right?" Dana asked.

"You know I will." Nathan dug into his pot pie.

"Either of you need anything else?" Ginger asked.

"I'm fine," Dana said.

Nathan swallowed and then wiped his mouth. "I'm good too. This pot pie is delicious. I don't suppose you could drop one of these off at my house for my dinner tonight? I'm probably going to be working late."

"I'll make one up special for you." Ginger winked and walked away.

Nathan and Dana finished their lunch and stayed as far away from discussing the previous night as they could. Ginger brought their bills and placed them on the table. Before Dana could grab hers, Nathan picked it up. "I'll take care of this."

"You don't have to do that. I can always turn it in on my

expense report."

"How late are you working tonight?" he asked.

"I'll probably head home around four. Why?"

"Keep your cell phone close. There could be something you might need to report on later tonight. That's all I'm going to say."

Dana got up and put her coat on. She leaned down and gave Nathan a kiss on the cheek. "Thanks." Dana left.

Ginger came up to the table and sat a large coffee to-go in front of him. "How did you know I wanted that?" he asked.

"Because you look like hell."

"I didn't get much sleep last night." Nathan laid thirty dollars on the table. "Keep the change."

"Thanks. I'll leave the pot pie in your refrigerator tonight," she said.

Nathan left and walked back to the police department. He was sitting in one of the interrogation rooms when Frank Bishop was brought in. "Hello, Frank. Sit down."

Bishop sat across from him, dressed in an orange jumpsuit and handcuffed. He didn't say a word.

"We found out who your boss is," Nathan said.

Surprised, Bishop looked up. "I don't believe you."

"We arrested Ricky Carter last night when he broke into another home on Mano Island and he told us that Mayor Newcomb has been calling the shots when it comes to the burglaries. Is that true? Oh, I forgot to ask. Do you want your attorney present for this questioning?" Nathan loved sarcasm.

"Has Newcomb been arrested?"

"No."

"Then, no, I don't want my attorney present."

"I take it I'm right about him being your boss then. Who was involved in Raymond Miller's murder?'

"It wasn't supposed to have happened. Ricky brought a gun. We weren't supposed to be armed. That's what Newcomb told us, but Ricky never listens. He's the one that shot the guy."

"Why did Newcomb want you guys to do the break-ins?"

"He needed money. He said we could keep anything we took as long as he got the computers."

"Do you know what he did with them? We searched the house where you and Ricky live and found lots of the stolen items, but no computer," Nathan said.

"He has a warehouse where we would meet him sometimes. He probably has them there, but I'm not sure."

Nathan shoved a notepad and pen across the table to him. "Write down the address."

Bishop scribbled something down and pushed it back to Nathan.

"Anything else you want to say?"

"Yeah, I want a new lawyer."

Chapter Fifteen

After getting the address for the warehouse from Bishop, Nathan called Daniel Grant and got a search warrant. He'd have to work fast to search the premises before anyone notified Newcomb. He picked up the phone and called Hank's cell phone.

"McCoy."

"Hank, it's Nathan. I have a search warrant for a building that Newcomb owns. Can you go with me to do a search it before he gets word about It?"

"I'll be right there."

Nathan hung up the phone and saw Sergeant Donnelly walk past the door. "Sergeant!"

He came back to the door. "Did you need something, Detective?"

"Please come in and close the door. I need a favor."

The Sergeant closed the door and then stood in front of Nathan's desk, arms crossed in front of his chest.

"This is a need to know basis."

"I understand," Donnelly said.

"We're going to arrest Mayor Newcomb tonight for spearheading the burglaries on Mano Island."

"Donnelly sat down. "You've got to be kidding."

"I wish I were. Officer McCoy and I are going to search a warehouse that we believe has the computers that were stolen from the victims. What I need is an officer to keep an eye on the mayor in case he gets word of us at his building. We don't want him to take off. Do you have an officer that could do that?"

"I'll do it myself," Donnelly said.

"Good. The less that know, the better. The mayor should be at his office in the City Hall." Nathan cell phone rang, and he looked at the I.D. "That's Hank. He's waiting for me at the rear of the building. Can you start the surveillance now?"

"I can."

Both men got up. Nathan headed out to meet Hank, and Donnelly went to sign out.

Hank was in his patrol car, waiting for Nathan.

"I think we better take my unmarked car to draw less attention to us being there," Nathan said.

"Good idea." Hank got out of his car and got into an unmarked car to head to the warehouse.

They saw no other cars around when they arrived. Nathan parked next to the door and had to use a crowbar to force the door open. "Watch yourself. It's probably vacant, but we can't be sure."

They entered the building, guns drawn, and carefully walked through the center of the building to the smaller office in the rear that Bishop had told him about. Hank searched the drawers of the desk.

Again, Nathan had to use the crowbar to force open a cabinet and there were the computers. With his phone, Nathan took a photo of the computers inside the cabinet before he and Hank picked them all up and carried them out, locking them in the trunk.

As they drove back to the police department, Nathan called Sergeant Donnelly to tell him that they were finished.

"Mayor Newcomb just walked out of City Hall and got in his car. He's driving toward Mano Island now," Donnelly said.

"Can you keep an eye on him? I'm going to go see the District Attorney about that arrest warrant and we'll need to know where to find him."

"I will."

At Daniel Grant's office, they picked up the warrant to arrest the mayor. Nathan called Donnelly. "Sergeant, we have the warrant. Where is he?"

"He's at his home. I'm parked on the street, just out of view."

"We're on our way. Follow us up the driveway when we get there. We may need your help."

Nathan also called Officer Avery, filling him in and asking him to meet them at the scene for more help. Running both lights and siren, Nathan got to Mayor Newcomb's residence on Mano Island quickly.

He spotted Donnelly sitting in his car and turned into the driveway just past him. Donnelly followed behind, and Officer Avery fell into the parade. They all stopped in front of the large house and got out.

"Ryan, go around the back of the house in case the mayor decides to leave that way. This isn't going to be pleasant, gentlemen," Nathan said, as they walked up to the door and rang the bell.

The door opened and Mrs. Newcomb stood there. "Detective Perry, what do I owe this visit to?"

"We need to see your husband right now, ma'am," Nathan said.

"He's in the bedroom. I'll go get him," she said.

"No, ma'am. I can't let you do that. If you'll tell me where he is, we'll go get him."

"Get him?" She hesitated.

"Mrs. Newcomb, where is the bedroom?" Nathan asked again.

"It's...it's at the top of the stair." She pointed to the curved stairway leading to the second floor.

"Officer McCoy, would you stay here with Mrs. Newcomb?"

Hank nodded, took the woman by the elbow, and then

led her to the living room.

Nathan and Sergeant Donnelly rushed up the stairs, guns drawn. They didn't bother announcing themselves before entering the bedroom to find Newcomb putting some clothes into a suitcase.

"Robert Newcomb, you're under arrest for the burglaries on Mano Island and conspiracy to murder."

Donnelly moved behind Newcomb and handcuffed him.

"I don't know what you're talking about. You're making a big mistake," Newcomb said.

"Read him his rights, Sergeant. Mr. Newcomb, I'd take note of those rights and not say anything else."

Donnelly read him his rights as they walked down the stairs. Mrs. Newcomb ran out to her husband, followed by Hank, who held her back before she could touch her husband.

"What's going on? Robert, why are they doing this?" she demanded to know.

"Call my attorney, Brenda, and don't say a word to anyone else," Newcomb said.

They took him out to Donnelly's car, where Avery now stood also.

"Take him back for booking," Nathan said.

Once Newcomb was in the police car, Donnelly turned to Nathan. You are following me back to the station, right? I don't want to deal with Chief Cabot alone when we get there."

"I'll be right behind you. Hank, you better ride with the Sergeant."

Hank and Donnelly got into the police car. Nathan followed them, as did Officer Avery. During the drive to the police department, Nathan called Dana. "Hey, you busy?"

"Just sitting here waiting for your call. What's up?"

"We just made an arrest for the Mano Island burglaries and for conspiracy of Raymond Miller's murder. You might want to get to the police station right now."

"I'm on my way. Thanks, Nathan. I really appreciate the head's up."

Nathan ended the call and put the phone in his pocket.

By the time Nathan got the car parked at the Police Station and went inside, it seemed like all hell had broken lose. So many police officers wanted to see the mayor get his mug shot and fingerprinted. Nathan made his way through the officers to the booking department as Sergeant Donnelly came out and ordered all the other officers back to work.

"Thanks," Nathan said.

Donnelly looked down the hall behind Nathan. "It's been nice working with you," he said, before he turned to go back into the Booking Room, leaving Nathan in the hallway.

Nathan turned to see Chief Cabot storming down the hall toward him. "Perry! Get in here." The chief walked into a nearby room.

Nathan entered the room, knowing he was going to get his ass handed to him. "Chief, I know you aren't happy about this, but I wouldn't arrest him if I didn't have enough evidence to support it."

"You're damn right I'm not happy. Why didn't you inform me before you arrested the mayor? My God, you arrested the mayor! You damn well better have probable cause because I will have your ass for this otherwise."

"I discussed this with Daniel Grant and it was agreed that the less people that knew about it, the less likely Newcomb would find out about it and run," Nathan said.

"This is the worst thing that could happen to this town." The chief paced around the room. "When the press gets a hold of the news, it'll go national. I'll probably lose my job over this."

"I think you're wrong about that. We solved all of the burglaries on Mano Island, recovered the stolen items, and best of all, we arrested all of the people involved in the murder of Raymond Miller. This could be the best thing to happen in your career."

Chief Cabot thought for a moment. "Maybe you're right. This could be a good thing for tourism for the town.

We no longer have a murderer running the streets of Mystic. Detective Perry, if you're willing to stay with the department, I will be making your job permanent."

"Thank you, sir. I would very much like to remain here in Mystic."

"Good. We need to schedule a press conference right away," Cabot said.

"Don't you think we should give the story to the local newspaper first? I'm pretty sure Dana Tyler is probably waiting out there somewhere," Nathan said.

"Let's go find her." The chief went to the door and out into the hallway in search of Dana. Nathan followed, since Cabot really didn't know the details of the arrest to give to Dana.

Before he and Cabot met with Dana, Nathan saw to it that Newcomb was completely booked into the system and in a cell. Afterward, he went back to his office to finish doing some paperwork pertaining to the arrest. A knock at the door drew his attention away from the computer.

Dana stood there.

"Can I come in?" he asked.

"Sure."

She came in and sat down. "Thanks again for giving me the exclusive on the mayor's arrest."

"You're welcome. I look forward to reading your story. How about dinner tonight?"

"I thought you had pot pie waiting for you in your refrigerator?" she teased.

"It'll keep."

"Actually, I'm going to have to write the story tonight to make tomorrow's issue. How about dinner tomorrow night instead? We can celebrate you becoming a permanent resident of Mystic again," she asked.

"It's a date." His cell phone rang. "Excuse me. Detective Perry."

"Hello Nathan. How are you?" It was Katherine.

"I'm great. We just made the arrest for the murder I've been talking to you about." He mouthed to Dana that it was Katherine. He actually figured she could hear Katherine's voice anyway. "It was the mayor, can you believe that?"

"I need to talk to you about something," she said.

He kept talking like he didn't hear her. "Well, actually the mayor didn't do it, but he was the mastermind behind the burglaries when the murder took place. We arrested two other guys for the burglaries and one of them was the actual shooter. Oh, and Chief Cabot made my job permanent. I guess I'll be living here permanently."

"Nathan! Let me say something."

"I'm sorry. What do you want to say?"

At first there was silence, then Katherine told him the news.

"I'm pregnant and you're the father.

About the Author

Carol Preflatish's interest in writing began in high school when she worked as a reporter, photographer, and sport's editor for the school newspaper. Publishing credits include several romantic suspense novels, two non-fiction books, and her new police procedural murder mystery series. An avid photographer, she has had many photos published in her local newspaper, as well as in Golf Journal, the official publication of the United States Golf Association. Carol is a member of the Sisters in Crime organization and Kentuckiana Authors. She lives in southern Indiana and shares a log cabin in the woods with her husband and cat in what seems like an enchanted forest with a menagerie of wildlife constantly visiting.

Visit Carol's official site online at: www.CarolPre.com